MW00476607

Leather Blues
The Adventures of Denny Sargent

A Novel of Leatherfolk

Leather Blues
The Adventures of Denny Sargent

A Novel of Leatherfolk

Jack Fritscher

Palm Drive Publishing ®
San Francisco

Copyright ©1969, 1972, 1984, 2011 Jack Fritscher

All rights are reserved by the author. Except for brief passages, quoted in newspaper, magazine, radio, television, internet review, or academic paper, no part of this book may be reproduced, stored in or introduced into a retrieval system, or transmitted in any form without the prior written permission of both the copyright owner and the publisher of this book.

All inquiries concerning performance, adaptation, or publication rights should be directed to the Publisher, Palm Drive Publishing at publisher@PalmDrive-Publishing.com. Send reviews, quotation clips, feature articles, and academic papers in hard copy, tear sheets, or electronic format for bibliographical inclusion on literary website and in historical archive.

This is a work of fiction. Names, characters, places, and incidents either are the product of the author's imagination or are used fictitiously, and any resemblance to actual persons, living or dead, events, or locales is entirely coincidental.

For author history and literary research:
www.JackFritscher.com

Published by Palm Drive Publishing, San Francisco CA
www.PalmDrivePublishing.com
Email: publisher@PalmDrivePublishing.com

Previously published: Gay Sunshine Press (Leyland Publications), 1984

Library of Congress Control Number: 2010938879
Fritscher, Jack 1939-
    Leather Blues: The Adventures of Denny Sargent / Jack Fritscher - 2nd
U.S. ed.
    p.cm.
ISBN-13 978-1-890834-02-9 (pbk: alk paper)
ISBN-10 1-890834-02-5 (pbk: alk paper)

1. American Literature—20th Century. 2. Homosexuality—Fiction. 3. Gay Studies—Fiction. 4. Erotica—Gay. 5. Sadomasochism—Fiction.

Palm Drive Publishing ®
Printed in the United States of America
10 9 8 7 6 5 4

for Bob Ehrenberg
and especially
Mark Hemry

Also by Jack Fritscher

Fiction

Some Dance to Remember
Titanic: Forbidden Stories Hollywood Forgot
The Geography of Women
Corporal in Charge and Other Stories
Stand by Your Man and Other Stories
Rainbow County and Other Stories
Stonewall: Stories of Gay Liberation
What They Did to the Kid
Sweet Embraceable You: Coffee-House Stories

Non-Fiction

Gay San Francisco: Eyewitness *Drummer*
Mapplethorpe: Assault with a Deadly Camera
Popular Witchcraft: Straight from the Witch's Mouth
Love and Death in Tennessee Williams
When Malory Met Arthur: Camelot
Television Today

Photography
Jack Fritscher's American Men

www.JackFritscher.com

Author's Foreword

Leather Legacy
The Sexual Infinity of Leather

I wrote *Leather Blues* for the pleasure of it, to capture life as we lived it. I completed the manuscript in 1969, and the novel has had a wonderful life. *Leather Blues* is a picaresque coming-out story of a roguish boy eager to learn the ropes, the rituals, and the sexual infinity of leather.

Because it was written a year before the Stonewall Rebellion, and fifteen years before gay book publishers came into existence in the mid-1980s, it was first published as a zine on a spirit duplicator in a limited edition of one hundred copies by Lou Thomas at Target Studio in 1972—under its original working title *I Am Curious (Leather)*. In 1978, it was announced as a forthcoming *Drummer* book, and was excerpted in *Son of Drummer*. It was serialized in *Man2Man Quarterly* 1981-1982. In 1984, Gay Sunshine Press published the first trade paperback of ten thousand copies. The text of this new edition is exactly the same as it was in 1969.

Readers and reviewers have ardently supported *Leather Blues*, which has been excerpted over the years in many gay magazines, becoming part of gay popular culture. Every author wishes for such enthusiasm.

Perhaps such a growing acceptance of boldly sexual literature shows the maturity of gay diversity at long last embracing the erotic literary fiction that defines our homosexuality better than does non-erotic gay literature.

Once scorned, erotic literature is now admired, and given awards for being good yarns well told. In our gay world built on subcultures, leatherfolk are the passionate few who have given pedigree to this novel, pushing it into the canon of the gay literary mainstream.

Leather Blues is a signature book that, driven by this passion of its fans, has, for nearly fifty years, stood the test of time which has encoded *Leather Blues* as a textual eyewitness of our leather roots before Stonewall. Its status as an iconic leather book, I hope, does not diminish the entertainment impact of its intended eroticism.

In revolutionary 1969, this seminal novel was considered erotically radical. Post-HIV, it seems even more sexually *avant garde*.

In terms of characters, structure, scenes, psychological flow, imagery, iconography, and dialogue, literary historians analyzing our gay roots, might note that *Leather Blues* reflects the 1950s-1960s gay zeitgeist of post-World War II masculine identity expressed by Marlon Brando in *The Wild One*, and by auteurs of independent films from the sexual underground: Kenneth Anger, *Scorpio Rising*, *Kustom Kar Kommandos*; John Waters' favorites George and Mike Kuchar; Andy Warhol, *Blowjob*, *Bike Boy*, the Velvet Underground; Roger Corman's heavy-metal biker exploitation movies starring William Smith, such as *The Wild Angels* and *Angels Die Hard*; and Dennis Hopper, director of the counter-culture classic *Easy Rider*.

These artists, along with William Carney's leather novel *The Real Thing*, John Rechy's *City of Night*, and my friend James Purdy's *Eustace Chisholm and the Works*, were some of the avatars enhancing my eyewitness life in leather. Generously compared by GLBT culture analysts and critics such as Michael Bronski and Ian Young to the novels of Jean Genet, Dennis Cooper, and Samuel Steward (Phil Andros), *Leather Blues* is gay identity literature representing gay male writing in the mid-twentieth century.

I wrote *Leather Blues* to be an authentic, erotic, romantic, psychological, and literary thriller, driven with scenes and dialogue that I tried to make as vivid and entertaining as the screenplays I admire. In fact, it is a movie disguised as a novel. Its scenes and dramatic arc are cinematic. Its "voice" is its dialogue.

The essence of *Leather Blues* is not merely the magical thinking of masturbatory desire so much as it is also a dramatized documentary of the way we were.

Leather Blues exists like a note in a bottle from the golden age of wild leather liberation before Stonewall and HIV turned mid-century gay sex into ancient history.

To project diverse perspectives within the cinematic narrative, I wrote the story in the "omniscient third person voice," not the typical "autobiographical first person" favored by most writers of erotica. My goal was to give readers "insider access" to dialogue-driven characters, plot, and sexuality they could identify with erotically.

In all my writing, I try to create erotic literature that begins in the head and works its way down. That reviewers have found the rhythms of poetry in my sentences, and male romance in my plot, and existentialism in my themes is satisfying because erotic literature is not written in an intellectual or emotional vacuum.

Respecting sexuality, I always intend my words and rhythms to turn readers onto their own sexual pleasure. My humanist goal is to cause human orgasm: the ability to worship something recognized as core necessity in one's human self.

There is no greater connection between author and reader than the reader's handheld salute to the action on the page. That's the best review in the world.

Leather Blues is perhaps the leanest, meanest, and purist book I have written.

May my pleasure be your pleasure.

Jack Fritscher
San Francisco, 2011

Denny Sargent, eighteen, kicked his sheets to the floor. In the fitfull ~~dark~~ hours before the summer dawn, his sleep grew lighter. He had slept alone in the secondfloor bedroom of this house every night of his life, except for his eleventh summer. One month during those hot nights an older cousin ~~*first*~~ slept stretched ~~out~~ spreadeagled in his wild sleep and forced Denny to the floor. Lying on the ~~hard-wood-of-the~~ roughout wood ~~flooring~~ wrapped in an old army blanket ~~hauled~~ pulled down from his closet, Denny watched the nightly ritual on the bed. His cousin, larger than he, with the bulk of a hefty sixteen year old country boy, ~~stripped-off-his~~ lay for a long while on his back, the pouch of his shorts mounding and filling, growing ~~with~~ something alive. For minutes the cousin lay without moving, then his arm, heavy with farmboy muscle, ~~descended~~ smoothed down the length of flat belly, found the hot coil tucked in the shorts, and kneaded the enlarging lump. Denny never saw what was growing in there. He never saw how big it got. The cousin always seemed to forget the younger boy ~~was-there~~ lay watching on the floor. Every night at a certain point Denny knew what would happen: the cousin put both hard hands on ~~his-basket~~ and rolled over on his stomach, hands and meat beneath him. Denny wanted to watch the older boy's face, but he could not see it. All he could observe were the beautifully rounded hams of his cousin's muscular ass as it worked up and down, down and up, in slow rhythm, making love to the calloused palms beneath it. ~~In~~ those weeks Denny watched ~~that~~ the ~~cheeks~~ of that ass, the way it looked good, tight and rounded, in the thin cotton shorts. Afternoons playing ball he caught himself watching ~~the~~ the older boy's buttocks squeezing and expanding in the faded and shrunktight denims he wore. Those afternoons he thought of the nights and the muscular ass pushing the large equipment under it into those sixteen year old hands. He and his cousin never spoke about the nightly ritual and when the month was over the cousin left with his parents and Denny never saw him again. At least that gave him his bed back permanently.

This particular morning Denny fell in and out of consciousness dozing and waking with jagged starts. Each time he woke he felt his hardon lying long ~~and~~ cool beneath him. His eye checked the clock. Once he touched its back to make sure he had not unwitched the alarm. The second waking from his doze he considered tripping out through his parents' bedroom to relieve ~~his~~ the usual AM pisshard. He judged his discomfort not yet worth the walk and dozed again.

In his sleep he met himself. He dreamed this dream often, and the plot never changed. He lay ~~big-as-day-sunning~~ naked except for a tight pair of faded gym shorts catching the summer sun behind his family's garage. The ~~small~~ outbuilding, ~~the-once~~ ~~been~~ now hardly more than a large shed, had once been a small stable and carriage barn. He liked the familiar view of his own body browning on the khaki blanket. He ran his eyes like hands over himself. He touched his cap of dark hair reddened slightly by the sun. Light down, almost golden, defined the lean mounds of his chest. The same neargold arrowed down into his ~~briefst~~ briefs. A ~~Snatch~~ of white untanned skin below the usual waistline contrasted sharply with ~~the~~ his ~~allover~~ otherwise even bronze. He lifted his rump to hitch the shorts up to the tan line he desired. The motion tensed out his thighs, arched up his generous basket.

In the dream his father slammed the wooden door of the old barn and stood over Denny, his shadow ~~cutting~~ out the sun. Denny felt ~~the~~ cold ~~of~~ eclipse. He opened ~~his~~ eyes.

Original page from the draft manuscript of *Leather Blues* written on a non-electric Smith-Corona portable typewriter by Jack Fritscher, 1969

LEATHER BLUES
The Adventures of Denny Sargent

Denny Sargent, eighteen, kicked his sheets to the floor. In the fitful hours before the summer dawn his sleep grew lighter. Every night of his life he had slept alone in the second-floor bedroom. Except for his eleventh summer.

One month during those hot Michigan nights, an older cousin slept stretched spreadeagle in his wild sleep and pushed Denny to the floor. Lying on the roughout wood and wrapped in an old army blanket pulled down from his closet, Denny watched the nightly ritual on the bed.

His cousin, larger than he, with the bulk of a hefty sixteen year-old country boy, lay for a long while on his back, the pouch of his shorts mounding and filling, growing with something alive. For minutes the cousin lay without moving. Then his arm, heavy with farmboy muscle, smoothed down the length of his flat belly, found the hot coil tucked in the shorts, and kneaded the enlarging lump.

Denny never saw what was growing in there. He never saw how big it got. The cousin always seemed to forget his younger cousin lay watching from the floor. Every night at a certain point, Denny knew what would happen: his cousin put both calloused hands on himself and rolled over on his stomach. Hands and meat beneath him. Denny wanted to watch the older boy's face, but he could not see it. All he could spy were the beautifully rounded hams of his cousin's muscular ass working up and down, down and up, in slow rhythm, making love to the hard palms beneath it.

In those weeks, Denny watched the peaks of that ass, the way it looked good, tight and rounded, in the thin cotton shorts. Afternoons, playing ball, he caught himself watching the older boy's buttocks squeezing and expanding in the faded and shrunktight denims he wore. Those afternoons he thought of the nights and the muscular ass pushing the large equipment under it into those sixteen-year-old hands.

He and his cousin never spoke about the nightly ritual and when the month was over, the cousin departed with his parents and Denny never saw him again. The adult relatives had had words. At least he got his bed back permanently. But this particular morning, Denny fell in and out of consciousness, dozing and waking with jagged starts. Each time he woke he felt his hardon lying long and cool beneath him. His eye checked the clock. Once he touched its back to make sure he had not unswitched the alarm. The second waking from his doze he considered tripping out through his parents' bedroom to relieve the usual AM pisshard. He judged his discomfort not yet worth the walk and rolled over.

In his sleep he met himself. He dreamed this dream often. The plot never changed. Always he saw himself lying naked, except for a worn jock under a tight pair of faded gym shorts. He lay catching the sun behind the family garage. The old outbuilding, hardly more than a large shed, had once been a small stable and carriage barn. He liked its look. He liked its smell. He liked the familiar view of his own body browning on the khaki blanket. He ran his eyes like hands over himself. He touched his shock of dark hair reddened slightly by the sun. Light hair, almost golden down, defined the lean mounds of his chest. The same neargold furred down into his shorts. A patch of white untanned skin below the usual waistline contrasted sharply with his otherwise even bronze. He lifted his rump to adjust his cock inside the sweaty jock. He hitched the shorts to the tanline he desired. The motion tensed out his thighs. It arched up his generous basket.

In the dream his father slammed the wooden door of the old barn and stood over Denny. His shadow shut out the sun. Denny shivered under his father's cold eclipse. He opened his eyes. "You out here again mothernaked?" his father said. "I told you a hundred times if I told you once, you don't shuck your clothes on this family's property."

Denny's body in his dream tensed its rump in reply.

"You got ideas you're so handsome," his father said. His own body was tight for a man his age: one of those bodies that was never really bad, but never really good. "I don't see no pack of gals hanging around you."

"Why, when you were my age...," Denny interrupted.

"Shut your sass insulting me," the Old Man said. "When I was your age, I knew what I had and I used it."

"I bet you balled every girl in the county," Denny said.

"I didn't stand in front of a mirror lifting weights and looking at myself. I worked real work. What's all that exercise got you? Shoulders and a belly no man ever got doing natural work."

Denny tightened his washboard abdomen.

"What you doing," his father said.

"An isometric."

"Ain't natural." The Old Man stepped aside and sun splashed over Denny's body. "Ain't natural," he repeated. "I don't want no son of mine up to what you're up to. And when I say it, I mean to back it up."

"Sure." Denny sat up.

"You may be a big boy," the Old Man said, "but I'm your father."

"Glad to hear you admit it." Denny stood up. He ached to throw a punch into the big man.

"I'm your father." The man looked him square in the eye. I'll tan you worse'n I ever tanned you before."

"Say what you think's been going on," Denny asked him.

"Don't know. Don't like it. By now you should be

bringing home some sweet young gal and showing her off to your ma and me." The Old Man shuffled. "Maybe you're just slow."

"About what?"

"Settling down. Your ma and I want some grandkids around the place. You be our only hope since Rick got killed in that war."

"Screw Rick!"

The Old Man flushed red and threw a punch. Denny blocked it and wrestled the older, beefier man to the ground. They rolled through grass and gravel. Denny watched his dream body scratched by the cinders. The rolling stopped, and always, Denny was straddling on top. He held the Old Man down with one hand. He slapped him with the other.

"Please," his father said. "Don't."

Denny roughed him up more. "Louder!" he demanded.

"Please." Red veins protruded in the man's face. The weight of his nearly naked son drove the breath from him.

"Louder!" Denny said. "I can't hear you, Old Man."

"Don't hurt me any more," his father said.

Denny twisted out of the strong old arms. The man moaned louder. His face was upturned, squeezed between Denny's sweating thighs. His face contorted.

Then in his dream and in his real bed, Denny felt the stirrings in himself. His father's mouth moaning inches away from his bundle of cock increased its sounds of pain. Denny twisted harder and his prick pushed hard against the rough pouch of his jock. The more the father's pain, the more the son's pleasure.

"I've flattened you, Old Man," Denny said. "Old, old, Old Man." And from the back of his throat, with full hawking force, Denny spit white flume across his father's face.

The dream always ended there although the sleep continued. Denny had come to expect its regularity, dreaming the dream sometimes twice in one night. Sometimes he felt guilty. But mostly he liked to see himself triumphant with his Old Man really getting what he had coming.

This particular morning Denny woke with the alarm. The last scene of the dream had not quite finished. That disturbed him. Anything unfinished always did. He shouldn't have let himself doze so long. He held his eyes closed against the bright summer morning. His hard cool cock tucked tight under his belly suggested a good mattress fuck; but afraid he would doze again and be late for work, he swung his feet to the floor.

He jerked his cock automatically. It felt good. He pulled its thick uncut sheath back over the head. A clear drop pearled at its tip in the morning sun. He stood and stretched. He smiled. Two days before, he had taken a young Mexican bracero at a highway reststop and fucked him in the bushes behind the comfort station while the young man's wife and children sat spitting Spanish at one another in a broken-down station wagon out in the boiling parking plaza. A worn *Huelga!* sticker stuck to the front bumper. The Mexican felt good impaled on Denny's cock. He had cruised Den so hard and with such innocent desperation in the john, that Den had taken him straight back into the bushes. The harder he rode the young guy, the better they both liked it. Denny shot into his ass just as the Mex pumped out his white load. Denny felt like he had shot straight on through the guy's ass and out his cock. What a sight! Denny pulled on his jeans and work boots. Too bad the Mex couldn't tell his wife what had happened while she peeled hardboiled eggs for the kids in the parking lot.

Denny liked the rest stop. He worked nearly every day of the summer at the service station under the ramp exiting into his small town. He had to pass the stop going and coming. He walked out into the upstairs hall. He had to walk through his parents' bedroom to reach the bath.

"Forgodsake, be quiet." His father's voice came from

under the sheet. On the floor next to his dad's bed lay a
Western novel and two half-hidden, well-thumbed porno
pocket books. His mother's single bed was already made up.
"You clomp through here every morning half an hour before
I have to get up."

Denny ignored him.

"Your mother's as bad. Been up twenty minutes fixing
your breakfast. Dishes rattling. Radio blatting."

"Same time. Same station," Denny said. "Same tired shit
every morning."

"Bastard!" his father muttered.

"Don't I wish." Denny walked into the bathroom, straddled the john, and pissed as loud and hard and long as he
could.

"That does it," his father shouted. "On my vacation we're
knocking a door through the bathroom into the hall."

"You say that every year."

"When I can afford it, I'll do it." The Old Man sat up
in bed. He saw his son's naked chest, shoulders, and arms.
"Christ you're getting big. Eating us out of house and home."

Denny passed through the bedroom not giving his father
a glance.

"Put on a shirt," his father said.

Back in his room, Denny rifled the old wardrobe for
a clean T-shirt. He found one at the bottom. Under it lay
two physique photo magazines he didn't want his mother
to find when she brought up his clean laundry. He cursed
himself for getting careless and shoved the books into the
false bottom drawer he had learned to make years before in
Boy Scouts.

"Denny!" she called up the stairs. "Dennis, breakfast is
on."

He pulled the T-shirt on. Its neck was tight and chafed
his forehead. The white cotton clung to his torso like second
skin. On each pec the tiniest peak of nipple hardened against

the shirt. He shoved the tail into his Levi's and descended to his mother's kitchen.

"We look healthy this morning." She pecked his cheek.

"Yeah," he said. He gulped his orange juice and pushed the bowl of warm cereal away. "Coffee," he said.

"Dennis." His mother stood over him. "You want to keep your health."

"Coffee," he repeated. "It's all I want."

She backed off. He knew how to handle her. His father had made her afraid of men. She tentatively touched his shoulder. He didn't resist. She ran her hand down his hard arms until she touched his big hand. She wondered how a young man so big could have grown from inside her small body.

"Don't stand behind me." Denny imitated his father's tone.

"Your father says," she began.

"My father says for you to turn down the radio."

His mother looked frightened. "I always think it's never too loud. Do you think it's too loud, Dennis?"

"If my Old Man don't like it, it's too loud or too soft or too something."

"Don't call him the Old Man," she said. "He's forty-two."

"Do I get any coffee?" he asked.

His mother stood timidly before him. "It's his coffee," she said. "Your father works construction hard to pay for it."

"I work."

"Your father says you don't give him enough for both room and board. He says you spend too much on your motorcycle. He wants a door to the bathroom."

"Who doesn't."

"And I worry about you too. All that time and money you spend working at that filling station and wearing yourself out at the Y. I know you meet lots of good Christian boys there."

"A guy has to keep in shape. If old Rick had been in a little better shape, he wouldn't have gotten himself wasted in Nam." He rewoke the memory of her dead son, his dead brother, to divert her. "Beside the gym doesn't cost me anything. I pick up a few extra bucks spotting older guys who don't have a buddy to train with."

"What's spotting?" she asked.

"Will you pour me the coffee!" he said. "Spotting is helping a guy work out. You make sure his elbows position right. Get him to breathe right. Maybe wrestle with him to warm him up or cool him down. If he pulls a muscle, you might rub it down with liniment."

She walked across the old clean kitchen to her stove.

The stove was her. She was the stove.

"I'm sorry, ma," he said. He felt something deep for her: something lost. He'd have left months ago, but the thought of her abandoned to his father had held him home. He remembered too well living as a boy under the Old Man's thumb. Now he couldn't say why he was sticking around. Maybe just for this summer after high school, with nothing better to do, maybe it was just for her.

There had been a day seven years before. He was eleven and that autumn his mother had taken him after school to shop for a winter coat. She had wanted to buy an on-sale jacket at Penney's, but he had convinced her they'd get a better buy at the Army-Navy Outlet. She had thought of her husband who had said the boy's last year's parka would fit well enough this winter. The next year he could wear Rick's hand-me-down. But Denny thought only of the brown leather bombardier's jacket he and his buddies had stared at through the plateglass window. They all planned to get one and form their own squadron. His friend Stoney named himself command pilot and barracks captain. Denny was to be head bombardier.

"This is the size," Denny said to his mother.

"That's too large, I'm sure," she said.

"The boy's probably right." The clerk spoke regally over the knot of his tie. "He really ought to know," the salesman said. "He came in here several days ago with a group of boys who disturbed the manager no end. We have such a problem with juvenile shoplifting." He looked Dennis straight in the eye. "And we always prosecute," he said. "I remember your boy particularly. He's big for his age and his face is more noticeable than ordinary. We found him actually wearing this very jacket in the shoe department."

"I was trying it on," Denny said. He didn't mention the extra fingers and touches the man had plied across his body as he took the jacket from him that afternoon.

"As his mother," the clerk said, "I thought you would like to know. He probably doesn't tell you everything." He shot a hard glance at Denny. "But we don't like unattended young boys playing in the store."

"Thank you," his mother said. "I'll talk to his father."

Denny pulled the jacket down from the iron rack. He slipped his arms into the leather and pulled up the zipper. "I like it," he said.

His mother looked nervously at the pinchmouthed clerk. "It does have windcuffs," she said. Then making an unconvincing attack, for a moment she stared the clerk in the eye. "Well, Dennis," she said. "We'll take it. That's what we'll do. We'll buy it right now. No sense shopping around and then coming back right where we started." Her eye could not again meet the clerk's. "I think this one will be fine," she said.

Back in the neighborhood, though the Michigan evening was late Indian Summer, Denny wore his brown leather jacket out to show his buddies.

"Take it and shove it," Stoney said. "Who needs a crummy leather jacket."

"But it's real," he said.

He could have taken them one by one, but all of them together were too much. One older boy with a light down of bristle on his upper lip knocked Denny to the ground. Another older boy named Russell, whom some of the boys who knew more than Denny called Rustler the Hustler for what he did downtown, kicked the fallen boy in the side of the head. Stoney pulled out his Scout knife. He straddled Denny's ass.

Russell yanked out his cock and pissed hard on Denny's head. The piss splashed on Stoney's hands as he slashed the back of the new jacket.

Enraged, Denny pitched Stoney to the side and kicked Russell in the left knee. The gang of boys ran off, but the knife had torn through the jacket back and the piss had soaked the lining. Alone, with dinnertime darkness coming on, Denny walked slowly home.

His father took one look at him and cursing sent him to his room. He fell across the bed. His wet head throbbed from Russell's booted dropkick. Hours seemed to pass over the voices rising and falling in the kitchen below. Finally his door opened. Light from the hall fell in an awkward rectangle across his bed.

"Take off the jacket," his father said. "It goes back to the store."

Denny pushed back into the bed, wearing the jacket; his arms wrapped tight around the warm leather.

"Take it off."

Lying in his leather, Denny glared back at the big man silhouetted in the doorway just as always in the dream he was silhouetted against the sun. For the first time in his life he felt strong enough to resist. "No!" he said. He folded his arms tighter around the jacket. He held the leather round himself like nothing he had ever held in his life. He had fought and bled in it. "No!" he said.

His father pulled at the jacket.

Denny would not surrender.

His Old Man pulled off his belt. He was a powerful man. The kind who worked hard from the age of six and was laboring at a man's farm job from ten on. He had tendons and sinews in his arms that knotted as he twisted the end of his heavy black-leather belt over his son. He yanked at the boy. "Don't tell me no, you pissing son of a bitch." He clawed at the jacket, but his hand slipped, caught the boy's Levi's.

Denny thrashed under his father's strong hold, but the man's firm hand pulled at the boy's waist, sprung the button fly, and ripped down his son's jeans.

"You asked for it."

Denny rolled on his belly to protect himself.

The gnarled hand, rough and sweaty, caught the waistband of the boy's undershorts, ripped them from his hips, exposing the boyflanks. "Rick never asked for it like you're asking." The thick-wristed hand brought the belt down on the boy's white ass. The hard lick of it raised a great pink welt over both smooth cheeks. Denny locked his hands together under his belly so the man could not rip the jacket from him.

Again and again the father struck the son until the boy's buttocks were slick with sweat, bruised with tiny colorations of blood. Finally exhausted, his rage at the boy for being younger, better, stronger, the Old Man stopped. He looked down at the soundless boy shaking with pain on the rumpled bed. His heavy construction boots had stained the sheets with road-shit. Grease. He pointed to the torn cuts on the new jacket. "It can't go back," he said. "You ruined it already." He stomped to the door. "You deserved that licking." His son's ass twitched slightly in the half-light. The Old Man felt embarrassed by a surprise stirring in his own gray cotton twill workpants. "Goddamn knows you'll be getting another before you get out of my house."

Den did not look up. His face and belly pressed into the bed. The door slammed and the workboots tromped down the stairs. In the kitchen the man's voice was raising, against that of the woman. She begged him never to beat the boy again. Then Denny lost the words, but heard the slap that ended the argument and brought her to tears. He heard his father's bass grunting as he took his woman on the kitchen floor. He buried his head deeper into the darkness of the old house. He pulled the covers and pillows in around himself.

The pain in his buttocks caused his temperature to rise under all the blankets. His chest and back sweated in the hot leather jacket. The warm smell of the new leather soothed him, lying hurt in his bed as it had protected him when he lay hurt in the street. The thick musk of it both times had given him the strength to endure. He knew wearing it he could take anything because it told him he was a boy, getting to be a big boy now, a big boy ready to become a man.

His hands, locked together under his belly, felt something new in the warm moist curve of his groin. The damp of sweat, the heat from the beating with the leather strap, the musk smell of the cowhide jacket: he was alone, abandoned and helpless before everybody. Until now. Now he eased into a way to alleviate the pain and the aloneness. Rolled into his leather, he was exploring a way never to be on the bottom again.

The jacket tripped his mind to the books he had read: of boys and men who endured the cold cabins of the lumber camps and the windbitten range. He sensed their toughness had a point beyond his father's. Their leathering into each other was rough but it was respect. They had become their own men. Tested in the raw, they pitted their lean muscular strength against the outdoors and against each other. They could take it, Denny whispered to himself. They could dish it out. I took it this afternoon and I took it tonight. I'm learning how to take it today so tomorrow I'll know how to hand it out.

His hands cupped around the soft warm handle of his

boycock. Sweat from his bruised buttocks, naked under the blankets, moistened the hairs beginning on his balls. He held himself, stomach down, as he had seen his cousin do so often the summer before. Once or twice since those summer nights he had held himself in this way, somehow searching for what his older cousin had found. But this time the leather smell, the beating, the thoughts of men who could take it from the weather and from each other combined to surprise him. His cock, always soft before, began to harden and rise in his hands. His heat increased. Sweat drove the leather smell to his nostrils.

Suddenly he was remembering a story he had read in one of his father's Western novels about a ranchhand captured by a railroad construction crew. The gang had stripped the cowboy, lashed him with a whip, then done something he hadn't understood, and left him, tied up spreadeagle, alone, arms outstretched and half-conscious in a railroad shed. He was the cowboy and he was the crew. His heat increased. The familiar flesh in his fist became exciting and hard. He rolled over on his back. The jacket creaked as he moved. The sound of the leather increased as his hand moved instinctively into the milking motion of a man pumping himself. With each stroke he solidified more and harder his manhood and his resolve. He was the cowboy who could take it. He was the construction gang who could dish it out. He was lean and muscled and hard. Each stroke moved him farther from his parents' house.

The leather-hide smell washed over him, raw as new-tanned skins, making him one with everything masculine. He became leather inside and out. He first knew it in the center of his brain when the leather realization for the first time went gliding down his spine, gathering whip speed at the back of his young loins, and sent him thrusting his bruised butt into the air. The blankets tumbled to the floor. His cock for the first time sprayed across his belly and hit the open chest of the leather jacket with the heat rain of a man. It was a new smell. As new as the leather. And he took his first taste.

It was his time. His first of a thousand cumings.

He fell back into the damp lining of the leather jacket, and for the first time that endless day he let out a low moan, one that neither the beating by Russell nor his father had wrenched from him. His was the low animal moan of pleasure. The welcome flesh-spoken groan of a boy who had met the man in himself.

No one ever saw the leather jacket after that. He had hidden it. And for the next two years, until he outgrew it, that leather lay winter and summer in his bed between his sheets and his hardening body.

Denny hadn't thought of those days in years, and this morning with his mother walking from her stove with a steaming pot of boiled coffee, he knew the time was coming to leave the house. For good.

"It's his coffee," his mother repeated.

"Then let him drown in it," Den said. He scraped the wooden chair back across the linoleum. "I'm leaving," he said. He didn't know whether he meant for work or for good.

"Your father works overtime tonight," she said. "But supper will be at the same time." She tried to kiss her departing son. He raised his butch-stubbled jaw out of her reach. She touched his tight waist instead.

"Take the bus," she asked. "The motorcycle is so dangerous."

He said nothing.

"I worry about you so," she said.

He walked out the screendoor. He lit a cigarette on the back porch.

"And the neighbors," she called after him.

"Yeah," he said. She couldn't hear him. "The fucking neighbors." He walked across the dew-wet grass to the garage.

"Good morning, Dennis," Mrs. Hanratty called at him. Her washline flapped in her azaleas.

Dennis ignored her. Mrs. Hanratty and her daughter, Madonna, were constantly trying to save him, make him back into the nice boy-next-door he had been to them *before,* they said, he had bought *that* motorcycle. *Before,* they said, he had *cycled* to Chicago and come back with *a tattooed eagle* screaming down his left bicep. Whenever his Old Lady and Mrs. Hanratty got together they plotted how to drop Madonna into Denny's way. "She's a nice girl," Denny's mother always said. "Maybe she'll settle him down. She cooks. She cleans. She can get used to the tattoo."

Mrs. Hanratty couldn't have cared less about Dennis. She favored the match only because she was one of the two persons who knew that deep down Madonna Hanratty was stupid.

The other person was Dennis.

Mrs. Hanratty wanted the girl off her hands. "I said Good Morning, Dennis."

Dennis ignored her and entered the garage. His bike stood clean and spotless in the morning sun. Chrome and leather and power. He pulled a soft chamois from a nail and dusted the traces of night dust from his machine. He had to laugh. The Hanrattys and his own parents all hated his cycle. And they were the ones who caused him to get it two summers before. He had been sixteen and working lateshift at a paperbox mill. They, and a biker he met at the mill, had both convinced him, in different ways, that a motorcycle was his ticket out. Out of everything he didn't want.

He had ridden buddyback a couple of crazy, beery times on high-school friends' factory Hondas and unmodified Triumphs. But that summer when he was sixteen, a lone outlaw cyclist appeared in his neighborhood. The rider had come to crash for a few nights and cadge a few meals off an embarrassed aunt and uncle. None other than the

righteous Hanrattys. The more noticeable the biker became
in the neighborhood, the less was seen of his relatives who
at his first arrival had been jokingly apologetic. In three
days they had become silent. They locked Madonna in her
room. They waited for their nephew to leave. They were
certain their name would never again be the same up and
down the block.

Denny feasted on the gossip. He watched out the windows. The man was shirtless, big-muscled, and hairy. Denny
moved like a caged animal through his parents' house. He
straightened the sampler over the couch that read "*From
Reaching In The Soul Comes Happiness Every Reach.*" He
felt the biker's restlessness to match his own. He couldn't let
the man take off without a word. He pulled on the greasiest
jeans, boots, and tank top he could find. Satisfied he looked
older and tougher than sixteen, he marched straight down
the alley to the Hanrattys' garage.

Lying back on his big hog, feet on the bars and chest
exposed to the sun, the biker smoked lazily in the summer
glare. Beads of sweat hung in the dark hair matting his thick
chest. Both hands rested near his groin. His cigarette hung,
a short butt, from his half-parted lips. Den walked close
enough to see himself reflected in both lenses of the biker's
mirrored shades. He could not see if the eyes behind them
were asleep or were watching him.

Quietly the man spoke: "I've seen you around." The butt
in his lips hardly moved.

Denny was startled. "I've been watching you," he said.

For the next hour they sat without much talking in the
afternoon heat. Once the biker, who had *SAM* tattooed in
block letters on his thick forearm, rose up, swept the sweat
away from under his naked armpits and wiped his hands into
his crotch. He swung his leg over the bike and walked up
the steps to his aunt's house. Denny waited. Minutes passed.
The screendoor opened. Sam walked back down to the open

garage with a beer can in each hand. He chucked one to Den.

"Thanks," Den said.

They drank in silence. Sam finished before Den. He crushed his can and tossed it toward a shelf in his uncle's neat garage. It careened across a worktable knocking a chip-toothed screwdriver to the floor. He walked to his hog and kicked it down.

"Get on," he said to Den.

It was an order.

Den threw his leg across and felt the widestraddle pleasant feel as the big bike settled under him.

Sam sandwiched his lean rider's ass between Denny's thighs. He kickstarted the bike with ease. He wrist-gunned the bike. It roared louder and louder alerting the neighborhood. Young girls peeked out from behind window curtains. In other rooms, napping in overheated beds, their brothers reached down and found themselves. Madonna, hiding in the bathroom, sucked her thumb. Her cousin terrified her.

"Hang on to my jacket," Sam said.

Once again Denny had the feel of leather. This time he was not alone. A man was in the leather. The bike exploded noise and exhaust as Sam gunned it down the driveway into the quiet old neighborhood street. They tooled past a group of whispering ladies.

What Mrs. Hanratty wanted to know was why Dennis was riding with a hoodlum who obviously tried to get innocent girls into trouble. "Nobody," she said, "who drives one of those dirty motorcycles can be anything but white trash. Even if he is my dead sister's son. God rest her."

Denny, for the first time in his life, didn't smile at the neighbors. He was tired of being the local good boy. Straddling Sam's bike, he finally showed it. He raised his fuckfinger in Mrs. Hanratty's face. He felt good. Sam's style was going to be his. Whatever it was. Wherever it led.

Sam's hard muscle and sinew moved under the leather as he shifted and made the big bike purr then roar like a huge animal under him. They raced out of the neighborhood wheeling like devils through the small downtown. For an hour they cut back and forth through the village.

Madonna, fresh from her bath, a package of new thread in her tidy little purse, thought she later saw Dennis riding wildly down Main Street. "Not my Denny," she said and turned dimly back into the sewing shop to stare at bridal fabrics.

Sam finally peeled away from the main intersection. "So long, suckers!" he shouted into the imparticular wind. Den started to slide away from Sam and had to grab both his leather and his barrel chest tighter. They shot out of town onto the highway. The bike spit smooth down the concrete. Wind Den had never known pulled free at his hair. The vibrations of the bike and Sam's leather body filling his arms started Den's cock rising. He felt he was melting into Sam and both of them were melting into the hot machine. They rocketed down the highway. Men. Fused together with the powerful cycle they straddled.

Sam yelled back to Den, but the wind took it.

"Yes!" Den shouted back into the roar, not caring to what he gave affirmation. Ready to give it to whatever this man asked. He pushed his face tight up against Sam's leathery neck. A mile later they swerved off the highway to a gravel lane Den had often seen but never investigated. A cloud of dust spewed up in a high flume behind their speeding bike. Den felt every bump in the lane. He felt the jars in his own spine. His arms caught the rise and fall of Sam's broad torso.

The lane wound back into some low hills. It became a two-rut path near an abandoned farmhouse whose outbuildings had all collapsed. Den wondered, without really caring, who had lived there and when. But Sam plowed relentlessly on up the path until it became a solid trail. Then he shot

wildly out across the open meadow, up and down the rolling hills. This first real time on a bike, his first time off the
paved straightaway, Den hardened into the unity of rider and
machine. Every motion Sam made became Denny's motion.
When the bike leaned and Sam leaned with it, Denny felt
himself pulled twice as far out. Denny moved with every
motion of the experienced man's body. Learning.

Sam roared up and down the hills faster and faster,
shooting the rims, bouncing Denny high into the air, beating the hell out of the machine. There was nothing on it he
couldn't fix. Finally, gunning down from the highest rise to
a stand of trees at the edge of the field, Sam pulled his hog
to a halt. Den sat clamped behind him, still holding him.

"Let go now, kid," Sam said.

"That was some ride," Denny said. He reluctantly
released Sam's body.

"Get off."

Den did as he was told. The hot feel of the machine
remained between his legs.

"You're okay for a kid," Sam said. He pulled off his
shades.

Den saw the heavy look in the man's deep-set eyes.
"Thanks." he said.

Sam laughed. "You held me tight as a lover."

Den turned red. "I think I got a little windburn."

Sam laughed again. He kicked his big bike up on its
stand and in one easy motion pulled himself off the machine
and stood facing Denny. "You don't scare easy, do you, kid."

"No," Den said. "I guess not."

"Like I said, kid. You're okay." Sam reached into the
pocket of his black-leather jacket, pulled out the butt of a
half-smoked Maduro cigar, lit it with a smart cupping movement of the match, held it in his mouth and expelled two
sharp long columns of smoke from his nostrils. The outline
of his protective shades was clear on his weatherbronzed face.

"What's your name again, kid?"

"Den."

"Den, old man," Sam said. He held the cigar gripped tight between his lips and hitched the crotch of his greasy Levi's skins out and down. "Den, old man, I tried to scare the shit out of you. In town. On the highway. On these back trails. You hung on. When you thought I said something to you, you yelled back *Yes* into my ear." Sam dragged on his cigar. His eyes narrowed. "Yes *what?*"

Denny looked at the man: chest bared under the leather jacket, crotch mounded, secret, and full in the jeans. His slightly bikebowed legs rose thick and powerful out of the oily black engineer boots. A chain ankleted the left boot.

"I guess *Yes anything,*" Denny said.

Sam moved in on the boy. His cigar still tight between his teeth. He grabbed Denny's arm twisting it behind into a hammerlock. Sharp pain made Denny wince. He made no sound.

"Yes? Even to this?" Sam twisted harder.

"If it's you doing it. Yes."

Sam pulled Denny's body up closer to his own. The pain lifted Denny to his toes, up almost as tall as the man who held him. With his free hand Sam reached to Denny's throat. He fingered the Adam's apple, adolescent and cleanshaven. The boy looked nowhere but directly into the man's hard eyes. Suddenly Sam hooked his grease-caked finger into the neck of Denny's gray high-school gymshirt.

He ripped the cotton cloth.

Slowly.

Down.

Teasingly down.

And off the boy's taut torso.

Still Denny made no objection. His lean body caught the sun. He was midway between boy and man. His chest and belly glistened with the light sweat of his heat.

"Yes?" Sam dropped the shreds of T-shirt to the grass.

Denny looked the biker straight in the eye. "Yes," he said.

Sam pulled on his cigar. Its tip glowed redhot. Smoke billowed out of his nostrils into the face of the boy still held tight against him. With his free arm, he took the cigar butt from the hard line of his mouth. He held it glowing in his thick fingers. Crescent moons of grease underscored each fingernail. Still the boy looked into his face. Sam moved the burning tip, threatening. Neither spoke. Denny's lean pecs tensed out under the pressure of his hammerlocked arm. If he moved, his shoulder would dislocate.

Sam moved the cigar away from the boy's chest. He raised it slowly past Denny's face. He puffed on it deep without direct exhaling. He lowered it deliberately past the boy's eyes to the left nipple. The smell of young burning hair stenched Denny's nostrils. His chest hairs were burning like needle fuses down to the follicles in his skin.

"Still *Yes?*" Sam asked.

Rivers of sweat ran between their naked bellies pressed tight together. The burning tip moved ever closer to the flushed rosey tip of Denny's nipple.

"Still *Yes.*" He stared directly back at Sam.

The biker flicked the burning butt away from the two of them. He knocked Denny to the ground. He stood over him. Both their baskets bulged under the jeans both wore. They had parleyed a silent understanding.

Sam dropped his jeans to his boot tops. His cock shot out thick and wide and long. No curve to it. Only the natural uplift of the super-potent male. Straight up his flat belly. The tip straight up past his hairy navel. "You don't scare easy, do you, kid."

"A real man can take whatever a real man can hand out."

Sam dropped down beside Denny. He unbuttoned the fly of the boy's jeans. His big motorcyclist's hand reached into the warm darkness. He grasped the kid's dick and pulled it out into the sunlight. The young cock arched up, out, strong and flushed. Veins ran big, blue, and smooth the length of the column. Sam was impressed. He said nothing. Usually kids this age he knew were all more lean body muscle than cockmeat. He squeezed Denny's prick. Nearly half of it overshot his big biker's hand. He squeezed harder. A pearl, clear and light-catching, appeared on the tip. The pain of the clenching fist caused Den to close his eyes. He dropped his head back. His hips rose slightly. With this advantage, Sam inched the boy's jeans down to the knees. Then the big biker dropped his 190 pounds on top of the teenager's body. Denny let out a small grunt as the sweaty leatherman settled down on him.

"You cherry?" Sam's hard breath warmed Denny's ear.

"No."

"You been with leather before."

"Not this way. Never before."

"But you messed around some."

Their two cocks lay buried wet in the sweaty darkness. Sam bellied harder into Denny.

"I messed around." Denny pushed up against Sam.

"You're not cherry. That's sure." Sam ground his cock hard into Denny's groin.

"I been in a couple circle jerks," Denny said.

"No fuckin' shit." Sam raised his unshaven face to look Denny full in the eye.

Denny spit the look back at him. Hard. "I'm not afraid."

Sam snorted and slid down on the boy's joint. That ended the conversation. The biker's hot wet mouth, tongue circulating, closed over the long adolescent cock. His well muscled lips pulled and caressed the blue-knotted veins of the young meat. He worked his head straight down. Deep-throating slowly. Then faster. With a neat little twist of his neck. He pulled up. Down. Twist. Up. Again and again.

His nose plunged on the downstroke into the moist young hairs. Sweat ran from his forehead into his eyes. The boy under him began to catch his rhythm in his hips, lifting and falling, his cock plunging farther down the big man's hot throat each time.

Sam middle-fingered beneath the crack of Den's ass. He felt for the hot dark hole. His finger, wet with cigar spit and dark with cycle grease, toyed with the fleshy damp undermouth. Denny moaned as Sam's finger teased ass in rhythm to the wet movements stroking his cock. They moved together now as they had before when the speeding bike had made them move as one. The cyclist had the boy up where he had never been before. With perfect rhythm, almost so the kid never noticed, Sam plunged his long finger deep into the dark innocent hole. The boy's moaning raised a pitch. In and out the finger played smoothly and swiftly while the cock grew harder than before. Denny's moaning joined the rhythms front and back.

Swiftly Sam pulled his mouth and his finger from Denny's body. His own organ was swollen, tumescent, red. He pushed Denny's legs, Levi's tangled tight around his boots, up to the boy's head.

"No," Denny moaned. "It's never been done."

Sam said nothing. He even skipped a good spit. No need. The lube of his cock had so wet his rod. He placed its thick wide uncut head against the rosebud opening of Denny's ass.

"No, please," Denny moaned.

Sam spread the lean cheeks with his big hands. His firm dick probed, then parted, entered the unstretched mouth.

"Yes," Denny said.

Both men breathed in short little gasps as they moved. Each working to accommodate the other. Inch by inch Sam's cock worked its way deep into Den's hot slick interior. They worked. They rested. They pushed against each other slowly. The man knowledgeably. The boy instinctively.

Until the young ass had swallowed the man's monster meat.
For moments they lay resting against each other. Denny's
legs were pinioned back towards his head by the weight of
the jacketed man's black-leather shoulders. Denny breathed
Sam's smells. The sweat. The cigar. The leather. He felt Sam's
buried fullness. Their breathing lengthened and fell together
as Den relaxed.

"Okay, kid," Sam said. "The honeymoon's over."

He knew what Denny did not know: the rest of the game.

He pulled his cock out almost to the head, then moved
it back in. Pulled it again almost out. Then back in. Almost
out. Then jabbed it back. He repeated the motion again and
again until the rhythm reached the ramming pull and drive
of a well-timed machine. Denny moaned. Loud. Louder.
Under the burden of the biker's body. This pleasure, this
pain was exactly what he had known one man ought to give
another. He suffered under the brute weight and cruel ramming, but he knew his initiation proved him a man. He
took the rite. He gave passage. He stretched himself further
to take more of it. Sam jabbed faster now. Like a fighter.
Shorter, quicker motions. Denny's grunts of acceptance
matched each jab. They were one. The trees, the field, the
bent grass under the boy's bare back fell from them. Cock
and ass. Leather sweat and boot grease. Respect linked one
to the lust of the other.

Sam crashed into Denny one last mountainous time.
The avalanche of his cum cascading down hot into the boy
triggered Den's own load, shooting it up high and far, like
some mountain geyser when the earth below is quaked in
two.

For a long moment they lay motionless. Denny quivered
twice. Final spurts of cum curled down from his hard cock.
Their eyes locked. Expressionless. Sam withdrew his rod.
Den sighed the long sigh of a slow withdrawal and his legs
came slowly down. Sam lay back next to him. He reached

in the pocket of his leather jacket. He lit a cigarette. He held
the smoke between his lips, exhaling only through his nose,
his hands locked behind his head. "You're okay, man," he
said. He didn't call him *kid* anymore. "You're quite a guy."

Denny knew that, knew it already by what he had taken
inside and out. Everything this man had to offer.

"What we did today," Sam said, "was for openers. Sometime we'll really go at it. You and me." He punched Denny's
shoulder. "You're new. You don't know what you want yet."
His voice trailed off. He ran his hard calloused palm from
Den's cock up the length of the boy's belly and chest to his
chin, rubbing the boy's cum into the soft down of hair. They
looked at each other. There were no words. They lay quiet a
long while.

Sam dozed, woke, stood up, pissed into the breeze,
hitched up his jeans. "Come on, buddy," he said. He dropped
his big cycle off its stand, mounted it, kicked the starter.
Denny pulled on his Levi's, straddled the machine, and rode
shirtless back to town.

Sam had made up Denny's mind.

Now two summers later, Denny had to laugh. Mrs.
Hanratty was standing under her morning washing. She
hated his bike and she was one of the reasons he had bought
it. As he hung up his chamois, before he kicked his machine
awake, he heard her shout to Madonna for more clothes pins.
Revving down the driveway he remembered how, weeks
after Sam had left town, he had trailed back to their field on
his own new cycle. He had found what was left of his torn
gray gymshirt. It lay sodden and flat where Sam had thrown
it. His bike always made him forget his Old Man and the
Hanrattys. But this morning it made him remember Sam.
He had never seen him again.

"Fuck," he said, pulling into the early morning summer
traffic. "There was a man."

Minutes later at the filling station buttoning the green

work shirt over his T-shirt, Denny refused to notice his boss had followed him into the washroom.

"So you're not saying hello to people today," Mister Martin said.

Denny looked into the mirror at the man's face over his shoulder. "I was thinking about people who say goodbye. People you never see again."

"Yeah," Martin said. "Get on out to the pumps, boy."

Denny took his time turning out the door. Martin thumped his ass as he passed. Denny ignored him. "Hose down the ramps," Martin ordered. He took off his wedding ring to wash his hands. "We're gonna be busy today."

"What a big fucking thrill for you and the Arabs," Denny said.

"Mr. Motorcycle Big Shot," Martin said. Only his unrealized lust for Denny made him take any lip Den dished out. "Hop to it!"

Denny piddled the morning away, working wherever Martin wasn't. Around noon he took the station truck out on a road service call. He changed the tire. The lady paid him, smiled, and tipped him too much. He drove off leaving her standing next to her car door. He was hot and hungry. He pulled off the expressway onto the sunbaked asphalt lot of an A&W Root Beer and chili-dog drive-in. He climbed out of the truck. It was a fucking oven. He stripped off his green service shirt and chucked it into the cab of the truck. The sun heated his shoulders and pecs through his tight T-shirt.

"Three chili-dogs with everything and a large beer," he said.

The high-school boy behind the counter looked out from behind his acne at the kind of guy he'd like to be.

"Yessir," he said.

"That enough for you?" The voice that spoke to Den came from down the counter. A business type smiled at him

three stools away, lifted his root beer, and spoke again. "I eat
a lot myself."

"Yeah," Den said.

"What do you know?" The guy turned toward Den on
his stool.

"About what?"

"What do you say?"

Acneface showed up with the dogs and the root beer.
$1.90," he said. He looked at the lean mounds of Denny's
chest and watched the muscles of his arms stretch as he
reached into his jeans for the change.

"Take it out of this," the suited man said.

"Forget it!" Denny tossed his own bills on the counter.

Acneface looked puzzled. He took Denny's money and
rang up the sale.

"Everybody else on your crew go to lunch?" The business
suit said to the counter boy.

"None of 'em eats here anymore than he has to," he said.
"You think it's great when you start, but after two days you
can't stand the sight of a hot dog."

"Never work around food, I always say. Nothing spoils
your appetite worse."

Denny bit into his second dog.

"When I was in college, I worked around food," the man
said. "I played a little ball too in my time."

Out of the corner of his eye, Denny watched him rubbing his crotch.

Then he looked straight at Denny. "But I never lost my
taste for meat. The tougher the better."

"That right?" Acneface said. "I like to eat pussy myself."
He said it so dumb and looked so stupid, Denny knew, when
the kid's zits cleared up, he'd end up being one of those hot
Appalachian men who drag their fat wives down the aisles
of discount super-marts searching for Blue-Light sales on
carbohydrates. Those guys never had it dawn on them how

naturally beautiful they were. They always had their pregnant pig in tow.

Denny picked at his lunch and toted it back to the pickup. As he pulled open the cab, the suit pulled up alongside him.

"If you can take a compliment," the man said, "you're a sexy guy."

"That so?" Den swung up into the cab.

"Are you too rough?"

Den bit off the last of his dog. "I can be."

"I'll just bet you can," the man said.

Den gave him a second look. The man's voice sounded like money. He might do okay some night. Better than cruising in the rain. "Hot today," Den said. He tossed the fish the line. He drained the mug of root beer.

The man got out of his car and took the empty mug. "Let me get you another. A guy who works hard as you all day better keep his fluids up." The man's hand slid into a tight grope of Den's crotch.

"No, thanks," Den said. And he meant both the drink and the grope.

The man pulled back. "You'd be rough with me? You'd beat me and hurt me? You'd pull that heavy belt right out of those denim loops and whip me? You'd tie me hand and foot? You'd fuck me?"

"I'd gag you," Den said.

"When?"

"Some cold day in June." Den started up the truck. "Shove off."

"Please consider me," the man said. He pushed his shaking hand into his suit pocket.

Den pulled shut the door of the cab.

"Take my card," the man said. "Come tonight at ten. You don't have to do anything but let me take your picture. That's all I want."

"Workers get paid," Denny said.

"Just a picture," the man said, "of my cruel master who is so cruel he won't even whip me. Take my card!"

Den threw the truck into reverse. "Jesus H. Christ," Denny said. "Whatever happened to normal perverts?"

"Think about the money," the man said. He followed the truck. "Just a picture."

Den peeled out of the lot leaving the man standing alone in the blazing shimmer of asphalt heat.

"You're late." Martin wiped his hands on a purple rag.

"Good customer relations take time," Den said. "The old gal will be filling up here from now on." He meant the woman whose tire he had changed.

Martin swatted Den's tight butt. "Okay, kid. Okay!" He turned back to his wrenches. "Keep pumping that gas."

"Sure." All afternoon Den chucked nozzle after nozzle into tank after tank. It was like shoving cock in asshole. He checked oil. He wiped windshields. He ignored the spread-knee muff shots some of the girls offered for free as they sat wedged in behind their steering wheels.

"Did you see anything?" a standard-option blonde girl asked.

"Naw," Den said. "Your oil and tire pressure check out."

"I mean that you liked," she said.

"Now where would I see that?" he asked. Her five-dollar bill was stuck in her crotch. He loved to drive them crazy. American girls! For some of the really beautiful ones he was the first time they had ever received *no* for an answer. It really blew their trump card away.

"Hey, good-looking, you want to see more?" she asked.

"I want to eat out your pussy till you scream for mercy, sweetheart."

"I can't," she said. "I mean you can't."

"Can't? Shit! You raggin' it, bitch? Fuck, slut, I'll suck you dry and earn me another Red Wing patch."

Her little foreign job roared out of the station, tires

screeching. Didn't even stop at the corner signal.

Martin stuck his greasy head out from under a lube job. "Damn fool women drivers," he said.

But Den didn't hear him. He was thinking instead about the lunchtime offer. He threw his oily windshield rag into a plastic pail between the pumps. A few pictures. A few bucks. Why not.

At ten that night Denny was zipping his leather jacket.

"You never take good care of yourself," his father said. "Late hours. Go to bed. Whatever you're staying up for ain't worth it."

Denny slammed the door on his voice. "Old Man," he shouted at the closed door as he back-stepped to the garage. "Old Man, I take better care of myself than you ever took of me." He slapped his hard belly. "You already had a gut when you were my age. You had to marry straight. To some mousey woman. No one else would have you." He sprinted his way to the garage.

Inside the dark building, with only the lights filtering in from the street, his was the motorcycle the kids in his old high school called the hottest bike in town. "They better believe it," Den said. He pushed the machine off its mount, straddled it, and kicked it into roaring life. His cock grew hard. He gunned the bike. Again and again. Exhaust roiled out into the moonlight. The revving explosions of the motor roared down the driveway. Echoed between the houses. A light on the Hanrattys' porch flashed on. It was the royal Hanratty himself: Madonna's father. Den couldn't hear what the old fart yelled. He only saw the paunchy figure shake his fist as he roared down the drive into the street.

"Screw all you little old ladies of both sexes!"

Once out of the quiet neighborhood, he swerved through the traffic, gunning and braking, lights flashing red and yellow for his slows and turns. He was his machine and half of what looked like breakneck chances to startled motorists was pure hardon show for him. He tooled the local A&W drive-in where he'd eaten lunch. Kids hung in and out of cars. They watched the steady stream of custom cars and pick-up trucks circle through the lots. They tossed used prophylactics into the windows of unsuspecting cars. They called it "scum-bagging." Denny passed a couple of his occasional bike buddies laid back on their cycles, feet on the handlebars, smoking cool and indifferent to the younger scum-baggers. He signaled them as he passed.

The clock on the Menu Billboard said 10:34 the third time Den looped the drive-in. He figured he'd made his john wait long enough and cut out into the street.

"Better quiet your rig down before you bring it back," the cop directing traffic in and out of the lot said. Den could tell he didn't mean it. He wore his tan uniform too tight in the crotch and the ass. His shoulders were broad as his blond smile. His police knee-high boots were spit-shined. Den had cruised the officer more than once. Sometime soon they'd get it on.

"Anything you say, Officer," Den said. "Keep after the scum-baggers!"

The young cop laughed. Den accelerated. He left him in a roaring blue cloud. Four minutes later, he kicked his bike up outside a row of new condos. The landscaping wasn't even in. He buzzed the name on the card, waited, ran his fingers through his hair.

"That you?" the voice from lunch said.

"Yeah."

The door lock buzzed. Den ignored the small elevator. His oily boots took the stairs two at a time. The door to the apartment hung partway open. He pushed on in. Immaculate. Everything in its place. Up against one wall hung a sheet where furniture had been precisely pushed aside. Cameras lay ready. The man was kneeling in the middle of his equipment.

"Lay out the bucks," Den said.

The man counted out a hundred in twenties.

"Get your camera working."

"Yes, sir." He looked up at Den. "Will you strip off slowly, sir?"

Den unfastened his heavy belt. He pulled open the snaps on his shirt. The man fell to his face on the floor. His tongue licked Den's boots. "Get up, pig." The man rose. Den made him pull off his bike boots. He unfastened the metal buttons of his dirty Levi's. He reached in and felt his cock. Hot. Thick. Juiced at the tip. He pulled it out. It lapped down over the opening of his fly. Its head was big and rounded. The circumference of the head grew bigger than mouthsize as Den milked the shaft.

Shaking, the man shot Den's picture. Twice, three times. All different angles. Den let his jeans slide slowly to his knees. He put his hands on his hips. His lats automatically widened. Neither said a word. Both knew instinctively the other knew his business. The camera clicked in front, then behind Denny. He pulled off his jeans and pulled on his black boots. He crouched down and the man shot low and three-quarters to the side catching the worn steel plate on the heel of Denny's boot right below the incredible turn of his butt. Denny grew restless. "Break time," he said.

Den stretched out booted on the couch. The man handed him a sheaf of photos. He brought Den a beer. "You take these?" Den said. "You're good." Den reached for the man's neck. "Get down on me, man." Instantly the photographer took the thick nub of Den's cock into his mouth. He teased and rolled the boy's cock on his tongue. His mouth filled with the flesh growing longer, thicker, wider. He had to drop and dislocate his jaw to get the hardening shaft and head into his mouth. Den was used to the wide-eyed glances unsuspecting guys going down on him shot up at his face as his growing cock began to choke and strangle them. He loved the sounds of their burbling. The sucking sound of their saliva. The involuntary way their whole bodies contracted when his engorged cock slid deep down their throats.

"Die, fucker!"

The photographer took more of the rod into his mouth. Once he stopped, dropped his jaw even father open. He swallowed another inch. His lips rippled over the veins distending up and down the thick length of Denny's huge cock. He pulled up, with just the meaty lubing head of the boy's uncut rod in his mouth. Holding it in his lips, he flicked the tight opening with his tongue. Again and again. Then suddenly he plunged his head down and by sheer act of will swallowed the immense length. Denny concentrated to keep from shooting. Nobody had ever swallowed all of him before. He cuffed the man on the side of the head. "Lay off," he said. "Save something for the pictures." He stood up. His hot cock pointed out and up, straight and true, at the tight pitch that raised its glowing wet tip higher than his navel. He felt like Sam.

The man stood him under a ceiling flood. The light fell from above and the right. Shadows spilled down Den's hard belly.

"You've good development of the Apollo's girdle." He traced his finger over the lower sides and base of Den's torso. He stopped at the root of Den's cock.

"Just take the pictures," Den said. "Can the color-commentary shit."

Den had the virtue of many big cocks. Once they get hard, and often even after they shoot, they stay big and mean. The man finished his shots. Den stepped off the sheet. He pulled on his shirt. His jeans slid up his legs like oil, but his cock stuck out with no place to go. The man eyed it hungrily; his buttocks contracted involuntarily in the slacks he wore. Den ignored him.

"Please, sir." He fell to his knees.

Den pushed him aside. He buttoned his fly starting at the bottom. He raised his cock up and tighter against his own belly with each button. Finally he fastened the waistband of the Levi's with inches of the cock protruding straight up his belly. The head of the cock he pushed under the T-shirt through which it shone like a wet crown.

"Don't waste it, sir." He grabbed Den around the knees.

"Get out of my way or get stomped."

The man released Den's legs.

"That's better."

"Please, sir." The man held the sheaf of pictures. "Take what you like." Den leafed through the folder. "I'll develop your poses tomorrow. If you stop back, sir, you can see them."

"Next week. Same night," Den said. I'll take these." Den pulled a series of two husky marines stripping from full Dress-Blue Attention to engorged cock-to-mouth and cock-to-ass attention. The smaller Marine obviously worshiped the large hairy sergeant. They both had hard muscled bodies and the sergeant's cock was almost the size of Denny's.

"Thank you for selecting those, sir. They're my best. I just moved back here from near Camp Pendleton."

"You do a good job on those pictures. Because if I don't like what I see, I'll waste you."

"Yes, sir."

"And one more thing. Keep your hands off yourself tonight. Next week I'll check. I don't want to hear you wrapped it up in your fist after I left."

"Oh, sir!" The man was almost crying.

Denny left him on the floor. Riding home on his bike, he thought of next week and what he would do. The memory of a scar, a burn, like a small brand, on the man's forearm intrigued him. Maybe, he said to himself, I'm just the guy to give him what he wants.

All that week Denny thought about what he might do to the man. He grew hot planning it. This is where I've been heading all along. Everything that ever happened to me from the Old Man to Sam has been pointing toward this. His cock inched down his jeans as he leaned daydreaming against the cash register in the cool of Martin's filling station. He wanted to whip and ball some ass.

"Denny," Martin came in from the service area. "Wake up. Customer out at the pump." He looked down at the bulge in Den's left jean leg. "Since when do you carry a flashlight in your pocket?" Denny hightailed to wait on the customer. "Wait," Martin said. "You can't go out there like that. Get it down or get it off. I'll pump the gas." He chucked Den's shoulder. "You young guys," he said. "What I wouldn't give to be that hot again. What my wife wouldn't give for me to be that hot again." The customer at the pump tooted his horn. Martin trotted off like a good little business man. Den glared at the man's back. "It's not what you think," he muttered, "Mister Martin, sir. I'm hot because I want to whip ass. Not fuck cunt. And tomorrow night I start. Tomorrow night I'm going to whip ass raw. Laid open raw. That guy's going to get more than he bargained for."

Martin headed back to change a twenty. "I said get it down. I ain't running my legs off all afternoon because you've grown a third one." Martin returned the change to the customer. Den followed his boss back into the service area.

"How about letting me cut out an hour early this afternoon."

"Thought you needed the dough to keep up that bike you're supporting."

"I need the hour more."

"Who's the lucky chick?"

"She peeled out of here yesterday. The blond pussy with the tits."

"She the one got you so hot?"

"You guessed it," Den said.

"She can take all that meat you're packing?"

"One way or the other." Feed Martin enough sex-shit and he'd let an employee do anything. "The old In and Out."

"Wowee," Martin said. "You guys." He wiped his hands. "Where'd you finally pick her up?" Martin wouldn't quit.

"The hardware store. She was looking for a good screw."

Martin roared and wiped his mouth. "I bet you laid her on the level and drill-pressed her with that big dick of yours."

Den looked at his watch. "In fact, that's where I'm headed if you'll cover for me till Wally shows up for the evening."

"Would I stand in the way of lust?" Martin said. "Go plug her, boy. Then plug her again for me."

God, Denny thought, what a fuckin' idiot. "Thanks," he said.

He pulled off the green service-station shirt with his name on the pocket. Outside his bike leaned in the shade. It stopped him dead in his tracks. It was beautiful. He gave it a good hard look. What he saw he liked: lengthened, reinforced frame, heavy duty clutch, oversize cam and valves, teardrop tank, modified gearbox, advanced spark, swinging arms. Every part of his bike was larger or smaller than its counterpart on a straight cycle. The afternoon sun caught shine on the exhaust pipes retreating from the cylinder heads, flaring up by the back wheel, ending in two trumpet bells a little shorter than Denny was tall. Midway up between the pipes the contoured black-leather seat began its sky-run descent till it tapered off up front behind the small gas tank.

"I built me one hot hog," Denny said. Thanks to some of the insurance money from his brother killed in action.

"Such a big hurry," Martin yelled.

"No hurry when I like what I see."

Den spit on Martin's scrubbed cement. He hit the kick starter. The motor blatted eager. Loud. His toe and wrist in perfect sync, Denny roared out of the station. His bike had always been an escape. Now it was a weapon. He knew it true between his legs. He envisioned the afternoon and the secluded field not so far off when he'd tie some guy down across his bike and let him lick chrome and taste leather. He roared through traffic. He knew one thing sure: man-to-man torture would be beautiful. He could make it beautiful. He could make the other man want to take what he wanted to give out. And what he wanted to give out was coiled tight as a spring inside him. He dragged his steel-plated boot heel around the corner to the block he wanted. He gunned the engine one last time and swerved into half a space outside the largest hardware supplier in town.

He ditched the clerk fast. "I know what I need," he said. "And I'm looking around." He walked from aisle to aisle. He judged merchandise. One after another he found what was right and what was adaptable. A hundred-foot coil of hemp rope. Four studded dog collars. A hard rubber carburetor hose, beveled. A bag full of wooden clip clothes pins. A dozen electrical clamps: point-faced and snub-nosed. That's about it, he thought. He felt like he was doing a juggling act.

Turning the corner of the last aisle, he thought he'd run into a mirror.

"Sorry," the guy said.

"Me too," Den was surprised. The other guy was dressed almost exactly as he was: greasy engineer boots, faded Levi's, sweat-pit T-shirt. But he also wore a black-billed bike cap pulled lowdown on his brow. He looked at Den's armload.

"Brothers?" he said. He held a couple lengths of chain in his black gloved hand.

Den hesitated, not catching his meaning. Then, "Brothers," he said. They both laughed easy laughs. They had more energy than words. "Picking up a few supplies," Den explained.

The biker reached for the black-leather dog collars. "Let me take two through the check-out. No use being obvious."

Den handed them to him. "How's your chain supply," the guy asked.

"Need some."

"Have the dude in back cut you two eight-foot sections like I got here. Less than eight's too little. More's too heavy to tote." He reached into a bin and pulled a dozen hooks. Each had a clipsnap at each end. "Once you make connections," he smiled. Again easy.

Outside at the curbing, the biker waited for Den. "Some chopper there," he said.

"Thanks." Denny looked straight into the cool blue eyes What he looked for was there. "Where's yours?"

"Around back. Smoke?"

"Pass," Den said.

The biker lit up with an easy motion. Den judged him to be five or six years older: twenty-three, twenty-four maybe. His face looked lived in. Good-looking. He'd been places. Those eyes had seen things they weren't fast to tell. He handed Den a small package. "Collars for your other two dogs. They must be big mothers."

"You like leather," Den said.

"I am leather."

"Games?"

"Reality. I live it, eat it, sleep it."

Den stowed his purchases on his bike.

"I got equipment you wouldn't believe."

"Try me."

"You want to see it or you want to use it?"

"Depends."

"We got to talk, man. Nothing's worse in the leather scene than for two unmatched types to pick each other up, get home and find they're both top men or, worse, both bottom."

"Top?" Den said.

"S," the guy said. "Sadist. Master."

"Bottom: M, masochist, slave. Gotcha."

"You learn fast." The biker pulled on his cigarette. "You been out here in the middle of the Michigan sticks all your life?"

Denny smiled. "Just tell me once the big city words for what I already know."

"This your first equipment?"

"Beyond my belt and my cock."

"You got it, man." He ground out his cigarette. "We all start somewhere. Guys tell me they're surprised I'm into it. Usually a guy comes out into plain sex at seventeen or eighteen. Then has a second coming out into S and M in his late twenties or early thirties. Me? I got an early start. Earlier than you. What are you? Nineteen? Twenty?"

"Eighteen," Den said.

"Christ," he said. "I'm twenty-five." They both stood in silence. "Come on over for a beer?"

"Sure," Den said.

"I'll show you some of my toys. S and M made plain old sex into an equipment sport." He spit down by their boots. "I'm Chuck."

"Denny Sargent."

Their eyes met hard on.

Their two hard hands met midway. Chuck wrapped his black-gloved fist around Denny's thumb. Den closed his fingers hard around the back of Chuck's hand. "Brother," Chuck said. "The right time. The right space."

"Yeah," Den said. He kicked down his bike and straddled it. Chuck clipped in behind him. The small seat pushed his basket hard into Den's firm ass.

"Nice fit," Chuck said

Den laughed. He half-rode, half-scootered his machine to the rear of the store. In back, he was surprised to see Chuck's hog: modified to be sure, but quiet. "Where you from?" Den asked.

Chuck started his cycle. "A week or so ago I was in Chicago. Before that Milwaukee. Did some time in California."

"Where you headed?"

"East. Toledo, probably. Detroit. Windsor. Who knows. I hear they got some wild lifeguards at Point Pelee Park."

Den had heard the same from a guy who had blown and sucked his way all around the Ontario beaches.

"Follow me," Chuck said. He pulled slow out of the lot. Denny single-filed after him. He felt he was following himself. Chuck gunned his bike. It burped once, loud, then shot off down the street. Den popped his clutch, lifted his front wheel off the pavement, and followed in hot pursuit. Chuck led him out of town on the old business route. They bumped down a double-rut path about a hundred yards to an old farmhouse. It was hardly more than a cabin. Both bikes roared together in contest, then died as the two riders quieted them.

"Some place, huh?"

"New to me," Den said.

"Nobody's been here for years except for a vanload or two of hipsters." Chuck lit the last cigarette in his pack. "I found it when I was out trailing. Searched for the dude who owned it and conned him into letting me bunk out for a few days. My leather scared the good citizen so he was afraid to say no. The whole time I talked to him he never took his eyes off me. Had 'em glued right there all the time." Chuck thumped Den's crotch a good one.

"No tricks," Den said.

"Come on in." The two men walked up the steps of the small porch. Anybody watching would have thought them a perfectly matched pair of hard young bodies.

"S and M," Den said. "Some guys must go both ways?"

"Man, you are new."

"Fuck it," Den said.

"Don't get riled, man." Chuck popped two beers he

pulled cold and beaded from a cooler. "Everybody's some-body's student."

"I pick my own teachers."

"Have a beer." Chuck thrust the tall can into Den's gut.

"Depends. My mood. The guy I'm with. Sure," Chuck said, "I go either way."

"Slave or master," Den said. "It's that easy to turn around?"

"Man, with some guys you want to turn around."

"I'm an S," Den said.

"So's God," Chuck said. He took a hit off his beer. "So are we all." He looked deep into Den. "There's honor in being a good slave. I started out as an M." Den flashed uncomfortably. "Can the judgmental disgust. man. Now I'm predominantly S, I'm a better S for it."

"I'll never lick anybody's boots," Den said.

"Until you meet a pair of boots you like."

"I'm total S," Den said. "I figured it out."

"You can lead a guy to bullshit," Chuck said, "but I ain't eating. Let me tell you. Out front. For every S there's a bigger S. Always somebody a little more S than you and when that S points his finger at you some night in some crummy bar and says *you*, you know he's talking to an M and that M is you."

Denny spit off the porch. "Always a faster gun after the fastest gun in town, huh?"

"Any Top Man who tells you he's never been bottom is a fucking liar," Chuck said. "And that's a fact."

"Any Top Man so far," Den said. "You forgot *so far*. And that, good buddy, is a fact."

"Never say *never*," Chuck said. "You always end up doing that exact thing the next Saturday."

Den poured out the rest of his beer into the dust along the porch. "So long," he said.

Chuck walked slow down after him. "Don't be sore."

"I didn't come here for a sermon," Denny said.

"So give me fifty lashes."

"Forget it," Denny said. "You been around more than me."

"Nothing worse than pretending you know all about stuff you've only felt," Chuck said.

"You mean that, don't you." Denny felt a sudden easiness.

"Brothers?" Chuck laughed that goddamn easy laugh. He caught Denny's thumb.

"Yeah," Denny said. "You said it." He'd never seen anybody in all his life he felt closer to. Except that faraway memory of Sam. "Brothers."

"My real brother started me out." Chuck said. "What a scene."

"Let's hear it," Den said. They walked toward the cabin.

"Come on in," Chuck said. "I'll lay out some toys while we talk. Beer?"

"Yeah." He sat down on Chuck's bunk and lit a joint.

"My brother was ten years older than me. He'd been around a lot before our folks were killed in a car crash. I was only fourteen and was a little crazy. I'd been in the back seat of the car. Anyway this uncle took me in. He meant well, but when I was sixteen and could legally tell the court where I wanted to live, I picked my brother. So he drove down from his farm, picked up me and one suitcase. That was early June." Chuck handed Den the beer and took the joint. He hit it hard. "Nice."

"Take a few more hits," Den said. "I'm ahead of you."

"I'd finished my sophomore high school, but I was big for my age and we both figured he could use me that summer on the farm." Den's eyes roamed over the leather jackets and a couple pairs of leather jeans. One pair had its crotch fitted with a black-leather codpiece. "He used to go off on weekends. On his bike. A run with some club. Late Friday afternoons one or two guys would pull into our lane and pull their bikes right on into the barn. He had an icebox for beer down there so they hardly ever came up to the house. He told me to stay out of his way weekends and he'd stay out of mine. But I watched what I could from an upstairs window."

Den lay back on the bunk. It was covered with a smooth black-leather sheet. He put his boots on it.

"This went on until mid-July. But before that, when I'd only been there a couple weeks, I was moving some furniture and found a key taped to the back of the chest in my brother's room." Chuck raised his fingers in Scout's Honor. "Honest, I didn't think much about it the first couple days, but the next weekend he was gone I tried a couple of locks. The key fit the bottom drawer."

Den's interest piqued. He thought of his hidden cache of *Physique Pictorial* hidden in his parents' house.

"My brother had some fuck books. Straight as hell. But he had some real man-to-man stuff too. You know, suck and fuck. He pulled at the joint. "And some pictures. Not magazine pictures. They were guys I'd seen biking into the barn."

"I've done some pictures," Den said.

"Not like this, man. In every snap somebody was tied up with ropes or chains. Closeups of backs and asses covered with whip marks. One group shot I'll never forget: five guys stretched up by their wrists hanging naked from a beam in our barn. Their ankles were tied and their toes barely touched the floor. You could see whipmarks on their chests and thighs. In the background, about nine other guys, half-naked in boots and belts and jocks, were going down on each other, or were watching one big dude who must have been the Senior S that session pulling a long rawhide thong attached to the tips of the five leather-bound cocks."

"Was your brother in the picture?"

"He must have taken them." He attached a metal clip to the burning roach. "Anyway, the pictures were real. None of that fake MGM shit. Those guys' faces showed pain. It got me hotter than I'd ever been. I lived for when my brother went away so I could strip down, put on his oiliest, oldest leather jacket, open the drawer and beat my meat. Those pics of that guy torturing cock! Drove me crazy. Every time I sneaked them I grabbed my dick rougher than before. I got to tying it up tight with rawhide so I couldn't cum for hours. Sometimes I felt more like the master and sometimes more like one of the slaves. I'd shoot and smear the cum that hit my face into my eyes and mouth and rub the rest of it over my chest and belly. I think that's what made me so hairy. I had a great time all by myself," Chuck laughed.

"I bet you did," Den said.

"It lasted about three weekends. I guess he saw I'd gotten into his drawer. I can laugh about it now, but the way those big guys set me up scared the shit out of me then." Chuck tamped a new pack of cigarettes on the trunk, peeled it open, and lit one. "There were six of them going on a run that weekend. As soon as they left, I went into his room, pulled the shades, and opened the drawer. I had about enough time to get my wang up to where you can't stop when they kicked in the bedroom door. Those fuckers were all over me. I fought them when I could see them. I could hardly breathe under all that leather and sweat. They pounded the shit out of me. It was like the picture had come to life. Their cursing. The crack and smell of all their leather. One bearded dude kept spitting in my face."

Den felt his cock growing in his jeans.

"In two seconds flat they had me on my belly and hog-tied. Hands to feet to balls. So tight I couldn't move. They left as quick as they came in. I was alone in the dark. I couldn't move. My cock was hard under my belly. I had already tied that up myself. The strain at my wrists and ankles ran straight to my balls. I pitched the slightest bit to the left and felt myself starting to shoot way up in my belly, but my balls and cock were tied so tight nothing came out. It all backed up and hurt like hell."

"Bet that cooled you down some."

"In about two hours they came back. I'd lost all feeling in my hands and feet and balls long before that. My brother rolled me over, still tied, on my side. The pull of the new position sent new pain through my body. He and his buddies stood around the bed. 'So you want to play games?' he said. I couldn't answer because of the pain. Then he motioned to one of the bikers. The big one in the group picture. He hopped onto the bed in full leather. Gauntlets on his hands. 'Answer your brother!' he said to me. He took hold of my cock and balls. They were swollen and purple and colder than the warm touch of his leather gloves. He squeezed it all hard. I heard myself moan like someone else was yelling for me. 'Do you want to play games?' he asked me. I was afraid to answer. He squeezed harder. He twisted my balls away from cock. 'Yes,' I managed to say. He squeezed harder. 'Yes,' I said louder. 'That's better,' he said. He shoved the four long leathered fingers of his right hand into my mouth and down my throat. The leather tasted of salt and bike grease."

"That's what I like to see men do to each other," Den said. He was rubbing his crotch.

"I especially like it," Chuck said, "when older guys work on a younger guy to initiate him." He opened a footlocker. "You want to see some of this stuff?"

"Is that all there is to the story?"

"Mostly. The rest of the summer I rode buddy on their runs. Some pretty rough times. They liked fucking me and I guess I liked them climbing on one after the other. After the first, it wasn't so bad. Weekdays my brother tied me up a lot. I liked that too. Especially when he'd go off and leave me. By the end of the summer I was sleeping every night in the barn hogtied to my own balls. When school started and it got cold, he tied me to the foot of his bed."

"Let's see the stuff," Den said. "How'd you get it here?"

"I drive a van. In it goes my bike and everything else I

need." Chuck reached into the trunk. "Know what this is? He held up an asylum restraint. "It's a thirty-inch waistbelt with a Lynch lock buckle. Straps on either side hold horse-hide wristlets tight to the waist.

"What about the ankles?" Den asked.

Chuck pulled out a pair of leather anklets. Both were fleece-lined and had medium weight silver padlocks hanging from them. "Good for shackling the feet together or for pulling them apart to a good old spreadeagle. Here's a couple pair of handcuffs. This one's a pretty standard push-through manacle. The other's a set of Mattatuck Handcuffs from World War I. It's got a single lock and can be adjusted to cause excruciating pain."

"Where did you get all this stuff?" Den asked.

"Professional suppliers. Medical resale houses. Auctions. A few sick inventor friends." He looked up at Den. "Hardware stores." They both laughed. "Get a load of these." Chuck handed Den a tiny restraint which fit into the palm of his hand.

"What is it?"

"A thumb cuff. I've used that baby plenty in public. Last month at the leather bar in Chicago this guy was cruising me all night so I took him back to a corner by the jukebox, slipped his thumbs in under this plate, tightened the wing-nut and with a small padlock through its eye secured his hands to his belt buckle. He stood with his hands at his waist all evening. Very effective and no one noticed."

"A good public start for a heavy private session?"

"Took him home. We hung on a good high and flew. I worked him. Then he worked me."

"Too much turn-about," Den said.

"S and M can also mean," Chuck said, "Sensuality and Mutuality. It's not always straight torture. There's nothing better than two guys together on a bunk. Sex is a celebration. A man and woman fuck and celebrate their co-sexuality.

Two women, their femininity. And two butch dudes, man, that's a celebration of masculinity. Ain't no man I know ever playing what straights think about our brand of sex: 'the part of the woman.' Hell, there's nothing like two men going at each other in full leather. Rolling and wrestling till the heat brings out the body sweat. Man, leather never smells better than when it's hot and sweated up. Rough sucking and fucking in a leatherman's bed is like sex nowhere else. I dig what men can do to each other in beds, bars, barns, johns, trucks, warehouses, woods. You name it."

"How about here?"

Chuck pretended not to hear. "I really rap on when I get high. Hey, take a look at this?"

"What's it for?" Den asked. "Opening up the ass?"

"Wrong end," Chuck said. He took the tool from Den. "It's an Agony Pear. It's historical. When it's closed it sort of looks like a pear. Now when you shove it into your slave's mouth, you turn this screw adjustment and the tongs of it curve open and up and the guy's mouth is held immoveably open. It presses down the tongue and presses up against the roof of the mouth. Beats stuffing the mouth with chains. Or jocks. That's great too. But with this you cut off the screaming. You don't have to worry about his breathing even if his nose clogs with blood." Chuck screwed the device to its widest open position. "The pain is intense. Mouth torture. And the whole time the mouth is held open, the guy has to drink whatever's poured." Den touched the cold silver instrument. "Comes right out of the torture chambers of the Spanish Inquisition. Compliments of Catholicism!" Chuck screwed the tool closed. He dropped it like a small bomb into his trunk of toys. "That's all for now," he said. Chuck stood up. From the bunk, Den was eye level with the leatherman's hardpack of balls and cock. He looked like he was about to split the piss-worn denim. I'd rather demonstrate the rest." He seemed to push his basket toward Den. "In a scene. What

say some night this weekend we cruise out together and pick
up a likely little M?"

"Not in this town," Den said.

"Precisely this town," Chuck said. "With the right
kind of come-on we can get everything from college boys
to young husbands just itching to have their asses spanked
while they're tied up getting what they can't get at home."

"What kind of come-on?"

"Leather." Chuck said the one word. He said it flat. So
matter of fact that Den knew everything he meant.

"Leather." Den said the word too. All his life had been
bound to leather. It had protected him as a boy. He had
made first love to his fist wearing leather. Summers, he had
worked and sweated with gristled men. They wore leather
gloves, boots, tool belts. He had ridden and slept in greasy
Levi's and black-leather bike jackets. When he was a hard
young boy, he had wrestled with Sam wearing leather. And
although he had never seen Sam again, the memory of his
sweaty chained outlaw leather came back to him.

Leather was the sign of the male. Leather was malehide.
Leather was *cojones*. Balls. Leather was cock. Leather was
stud. Leather was men sweating, primal, growing large and
hard on each other. Leather was a gag working on a chained
initiate. Pissing into the leather lining. Pouring motor oil
over the leather britches. Leather was sound, taste, smell.
Leather was pleasure. Leather was pain. Leather was tying
and being tied. Leather was whipping and being whipped.
His skin was leather. Chest-to-chest or back-to-belly, leather
moving against leather was the feel, the celebration of mansex. To become leather was to see that nothing else mat-
tered. To become leather a guy leaves everything else behind.
Den was hard leather, hard muscle, hard cock. Nothing else
would ever count as much. When a guy wears leather he
gives the finger to the world.

"Is the cruising a deal?" Chuck asked.

Den sprang from the bed and jumped the biker. He wrapped his arms tight around the big muscled man.

"Then it's a deal, brother," Chuck said as they tumbled down in a spill of denim and leather and boots across the bunk.

Hard-muscled grip met hard-muscled grip. Their arms strained in athletic embrace. Den's knee dropped a slightly pulled kick into Chuck's enlarging groin. Chuck fell back on the bunk. Den took the advantage. He straddled Chuck's tight belly and reached down to the base of the pinioned man's neck. Branches of veins strained from under Chuck's strong chin down to the neck of his T-shirt. A shock of black chest hair tufted over the lip of the shirt. Den reached to the spot. He took a hard handful of the cotton material and in one savage motion shredded Chuck's shirt from his body. The man on the bottom grunted as the material broke at the base of his throat. Den tossed the white rag of shirt to the floor. Chuck lay back with his eyes closed. His thick chest rose and fell from the exertion of their struggle. Red-black hair defined his huge pecs. Den judged it the perfect marking. The hair, coarse and tight, stopped just below the nipple line. Each tit stood up hard, pink, expectant. The belly was strong, rippled, and hairless. Three inches above the navel, belly hair corkscrewed over the man's low-slung black-leather belt. Den felt beads of sweat under his own arms begin running down the inside traces of his biceps. His own T-shirt clung in widening sweat circles high up both his sides. It was the wet cotton smell of clean cotton T-shirts and fresh washed jocks breaking into ripe new sweat. His shirt clung wet to the flesh and muscle of his spreading lats.

In sudden turnabout, Chuck reached up to Den who was straddling him like a hot bike. In a motion equal to Denny's own, his strong right hand, each fingernail of it crescented with irremovable grease moons, ripped down Denny's shirt, open neck to navel. A halfbreed ring of quartz and copper on Chuck's hand grazed Den's belly raising a fast thin line of blood. Den fell hard across the prone man. The boniness of their jaws, roughed out with an unshaven day's growth, met as Den put his tight lips against Chuck's ear. "I'll waste you for that," he said.

Chuck planted his grease blackened boots on the leather bunk. His knees shot up. His hips arched. In a second he had flipped Denny to the underside. The younger rider lay flat on his belly. The denim-bound mounds of his ass tucked neatly between Chuck's thighs. Chuck leaned forward to twist Den's arm back and up against his sweat-slicked shoulder.

He pressed his basket against Den's warm ass. His cock bucked up in his jeans. He moved it like a dowser's rod over the dark, moist hole of Den's upturned ass. Months of hard biking had pounded Denny's cheeks full and tight. Chuck knew it was the perfect ass for his leathercock. He reached under Den's belly, still astraddle him, worked open his leather belt, and popped the metal buttons of Den's fly. He twisted Den's arm farther up his back to raise his ass and strip down the Levi's.

But Denny had other ideas.

As his jeans slipped down his legs, Den took advantage of Chuck's raised straddle and flipped himself over. He lay on his back under the top rider. Chuck looked surprised down into Den's face. "I'm a front man," Den said. "I don't take it in the ass."

Chuck grabbed Den's thick cock into both his hands. He squeezed it hard. Den arched in pain. He groaned. "That's it, man," Chuck said. "Let's hear it. I want to hear you talking with your cock. Fucking enough of you talking with your mouth." He squeezed it harder. "I want to hear you sounding like you have a man on you." He wrenched Den's big bar of cock. Den moaned again. His eyes closed. He smelled the greased leather and he remembered that long fucking-gone Sam. Sweat from Chuck's forehead dripped on Den's chest.

Salt stung the ring scratch. Blood from the tiny line mixed with the sweat and ran into the washboard crevices of his belly.

Chuck pulled the skin of Den's cock up so far it formed new lips around the big uncircumcised head. Den made no sound, but his face contorted. Chuck's own rod stretched farther in his jeans. He winced as his doubling meat pushed against his skintight denim seeking room to grow larger. With his right hand he mauled Den's cock. With his left he counter-massaged Den's balls. He pulled cock one way, balls the other.

Den's head rolled left and right. Chuck, like Sam, was a river he could float away on. He was back in the field with Sam, his legs again up over his head, hurting under the cock-ramming stabs of the cursing and sweaty leatherman. Den had found good sex since; but this time, this way, with Chuck was the best since Sam. He knew he'd have to fake any sex short of leather sex after this.

Chuck halted his two-handed twisting. Den felt a circle of rawhide draw tight around the base of his balls. "No," he said. "Take it," Chuck ordered. He drew the long piece of rawhide under, between, and then tight against the base of Den's cock. His balls were separated from each other and the pair of separated balls from his cock. The leather was castrating him. The pressure of the binding tightened the skin so that the veins in the nuts pushing apart purpled like tiny starburst explosions on the surface of Den's taut scrotum. He moaned. Chuck wrapped the rawhide tighter around the base of Den's cock. He floated deeper down the river. His already immense organ stretched its juicy tip still farther up. Chuck unbuttoned his own fly. His cock was too big and hard to manipulate out the opening. He stood on the bunk. Den opened his eyes to see the commanding man standing over him. Chuck's boots pressed tight against Den's hips. He unbuckled his belt. Den saw his hand slip menacingly into his jeans. He dug in and under handing out his cock. On its own his raw meat popped up and out from the constricting darkness of the jeans and the help of the hand. In its new freedom it grew another inch, high over Den's laid-back body. Chuck pulled another leather jacket from its hook over the bunk. It had been his first, a gift to him from his brother and his brother's club buddies.

The night they gave it to him he had been stripped and bound to rings on the barn floor. In a gang circle, towering over him, all eleven men had one by one, then together, pissed all over him. His brother's stream gushed hard against his lips until finally he parted his lips and his brother's piss strained through his teeth. The other men urged his brother on and their urgency caused Chuck to part his teeth. He opened his mouth. Full. His brother pissed harder. His cheeks filled. "Drink it," his brother ordered. Chuck's eyes went wild. The groups closed in tighter. He swallowed. They cheered. He gagged. They called for more. He swallowed. Once. Twice. And then his separate swallows became drinking as he took gulp after gulp of his older brother's strong piss.

His newfound thirst excited them. One shot his load into Chuck's wet face. Then several at a time came on him. Piss and cum mixed and ran from his body. His brother finished his long healthy piss. His cock hardened. He lowered it slowly to Chuck's wet mouth and thrust it deep down his piss-primed throat. He fucked deep. Chuck was choking. He fucked deeper. Chuck's eyes widened as the cock cut his breathing sharply under the thrusting weight of his brother's hips. Planted that deep, his brother came in long thrusts.

They were suddenly more than brothers.

His brother held his cock in place in his mouth. Another man went down on Chuck's own cock. He licked off the shaft, the piss and cum of the group, and sucked fast and neat taking Chuck's virgin load.

They had a good laugh at how fast he came. They untied him immediately. They pulled him to his feet. He was shiny wet. Cum and piss dripped from his hair to his shoulders. It ran down his belly. It wet the back of his legs. They wrapped the new black-leather jacket around him. They hugged him. Goosed him. Shook his hand. The black leather was their present on his baptism as one of them.

As far as Chuck knew, this was Denny's initiation into leather sex. That jacket was the jacket to wear. He slipped his muscled arms into the leather and dropped to his knees over Denny. Den felt the hot hard ram of Chuck's cock stab into his belly. Then Chuck stretched full length on top of Den. Their mixed sweat and the rich wet of Den's blood dampened the leather. Its rich musk crazed them both. They pitched and rolled over one another. Den's bound cock and balls grew tighter with each slap against Chuck's free swinging package. Their bellies and chests slid across sheets of sweat. Chuck pulled an inhaler from his jacket pocket. He shoved the fresh-popped amyl up Den's left nostril. His greasy thumb held closed the right. Den pulled heavy on the popper. He breathed three great gulps of it before Chuck pulled away the inhaler draining the rest himself. Den's face reddened. He fell back on the bunk.

Chuck reared up when the amyl charge hit his brain. He fell in a fury of lust on Den's body. He ground his cock into Den's tied pouch. Both of them were spinning down long black corridors toward a pinpoint of purple light somewhere behind their pituitaries. Den moaned. Chuck's weight crushed the breath out of him. They thrashed together on the edge of orgasm. Minutes passed. They pulled back. They crashed into each other. The sweat ran between them rich and hot. Chuck pulled himself up over Den. His lips curled into a dark smile. Slowly and methodically, both of them wincing in the manpain, he tied the head of his cock tight to the base of Den's. Their rods matched evenly enough that he wrapped the head of Denny's dick securely against the hairy root of his own. The double pinches of pain stopped them for seconds. Their separate breathing fell rhythmically together. Chuck hovered over Den. He supported himself on his arms. Then with one hand he hit them both with more popper. Neither man pitched or rolled this time; they relaxed into the leather pain of their tied cocks. "We are one in leather," Chuck said.

"What?" Den asked. The bloodbrain explosions of the popper were all he could hear. The roar.

"Brothers," Chuck said.

Den repeated the word. "Brothers," he whispered. His voice was hoarse, dried by the amyl.

Chuck reached down and with a new length of rawhide wrapped the two cocks together. Both rods were completely bound together by the rough leather. Chuck eased himself down on top of Den. The slow descent of his body was critical: the beginning descent of every push-up ever pumped out in any gym. The cockhead of the one jabbed into the cockroots of the other. Den felt his cock being wrenched slowly apart as Chuck descended down on his body. Their flat bellies tensed together. For a long while they lay tied together. Their breathing stayed in tight step. Den had no idea of time. Then Chuck stirred. He pulled more popper from his leather. As they came down from one, he hit them with another. Their high pounded on. Den writhed under Chuck. Chuck twisted in the pleasure of pain on top of Den. Finally he threw the inhaler to the floor. He quickly popped two capsules and shoved the yellow mesh bags between their noses. He pushed his wet mouth hard against Den's. Both men inhaled deeply. Chuck's wet tongue probed Den's lips, snapped through his teeth, deep back into his mouth. Their bodies contorted. They pulled apart and crashed together. Den bucked so strong that Chuck's body rose high off the bunk then fell heavy as a tackler back on the body below.

They made animal sounds. Their cocks stretched and pulled at each other. The mutual torture was exquisite. Then almost at the same moment each man's load started its run down from his pituitary, along his spine, to the bloodwild cocks. When the hot streams of seed reached the tied organs, they stopped, surprised by the channels bound shut with leather strips. Each man's rod convulsed in dry orgasm. Both felt the intense pleasure of sensual pain as their choked organs pulled together and the hot wet lustseed backed up into their bellies, turned back in its hot wake, back to the tied cocks, burning to escape. Whirlpools of cum crashed at the base of their bodies. The wild spasms of their dry cuming together lasted on beyond the longest time either had ever cum wet before. Finally they came to rest on one another. The fury of their pleasure spent. Chuck knocked the dead poppers to the floor. For long minutes they lay panting chest to chest.

When their breathing steadied, Chuck's dried voice rasped into Denny's ear. "You okay?"

"Yeah."

"Good," Chuck said. "You got a treat coming yet." Chuck sat up. The new distribution of his weight caused Den to moan. "Easy," he said. He pulled a mashed pair of black-leather gloves from another pocket. He balled them both up and shoved one into Den's mouth. "Hold on, man," he said. "One final number."

Den opened his eyes quick enough to see Chuck shove the other glove into his own mouth. Then with gritted determination, Chuck yanked open the slip knot of rawhide. Faster and faster he unraveled the bound cocks. Den bit hard into the greasy glove. Both felt excruciating pain as warm feeling flowed into their hard-frozen cocks. They were enduring. The backed-up rivers of seed swirled once, then flowed fast, milkwhite, shooting down their seminal vesicles, gorging out their flushed cocks. Again and again they bellied into each other. Hard cocks met smooth muscled skin. They pumped load after load of cum into the pool of sweat and blood between them. Then for the last time Chuck fell to rest on top of Den. They lay in athletic embrace. Each man took the measure of the other. They had endured. Finally Chuck raised his head up. The strong line of his chin hung like a cliff over the jutting straight jaw of his partner. Eye to eye.

"How was that?" Chuck asked.

"Brothers," Den said. He punched his buddy's back.

Chuck laughed and rolled off Den. They lay side by side. The night air was cool on their bellies. Den sat up and watched the early moon spilling in through the cabin windows. It lit the cumshine on their breathing bellies. Out on the highway, they heard the traffic roaring by. Several trucks rumbled down the pavement into the darkness. But the sound they attended to most was the outlaw doppler *whineroarwhine* of lone cycles tearing down the stretches of lonely road. Some of them hot with their machines boiling between their legs.

It was over for the night. Den knew it. Chuck knew it. The time and space between them mellowed. Chuck sat up, threw his legs over the edge of the bed, and lit a cigarette. He coughed and swore lightly. "Damn poppers." He rose and wiped his belly with the rag of his torn T-shirt. He tossed the sticky cloth to Den who mopped himself dry. "It's late," Chuck said. "How about a beer?" Den gave him a silent thumbs-up. Chuck popped the cans. They both pulled hard at the cool beer. Den chugged. Chuck followed. They laughed. Their Levi's were again up tight against their bodies. Their boots crushed the broken mesh of the used poppers. Chuck pulled a faded sweatshirt minus sleeves from his trunk. "Wear this home," he said.

Den pulled the gray cotton over his head. He smelled the leatherscent, the mansmell of his new brother. "About tomorrow night," he said.

"Yeah?" Chuck said. He popped them each another beer.

"You get your equipment ready and I'll deliver us an M at eleven o'clock."

"You said there was no such animal in this town."

"Until this week. A new guy's moved in. Transferred here from San Francisco. At least I got that impression."

"That's a hot impression to get." Chuck said. "Be here at eleven. I'll set the scene."

The two men walked to the porch of the cabin. This time Den took Chuck's thumb in tight grip. "We made it, man," Den said.

Chuck looked straight at him. "I never doubted but that we would."

Den stepped off the porch, tossed his quarter-full beer can high off into the moonlight. Beer streamed down from it as it sailed silver out into the bushes.

"Keeping America beautiful," Chuck said. His beer can hung from his right hand down by his thigh. His other hand rubbed back and forth on the grease-matted hair of his high chest.

Den knocked down his bike, straddled it, and kicked it alive. For a moment he stood holding it roaring between his legs. "You okay?" he yelled at the leatherman on the porch.

Chuck said nothing. But Den could see his large smile in the dark. Then the man's arm came out of porchshadow: flexed, graceful, thumbs-up. That was enough for Den. He roared around in a circle before the cabin. Once, twice, roiling up clouds of dust in the moonlight. Then he gunned down the lane. Chuck watched the headlight beam of the bike jump crazily over the bumps in the path. For a moment the bike hesitated where the lane met the shoulder of the highway. Then came a loud roar as Den gunned the bike and cut into the traffic speeding down the concrete ribbon into the small city.

Later that same night, Denny's father wanted to know where he had been. Denny refused to answer. His mother

began crying as the older man yelled at his son. She tried
to stuff back into Den's bureau drawers the clothes the Old
Man was throwing to the floor.

Den stood cool and apart.

His father turned his wrath on the crying woman. Den,
standing in denim and leather in the room where he had
slept as a boy, felt the mansweat rolling down the inside of
his thick arms. He felt apart from them. For the first time.
He saw it was their fight. They enjoyed it. They had put
him in the middle like some military objective. But now he
was no longer under them. He pulled a pack of cigarettes
from his leather jacket; he lit the smoke. Again the leather
touched his essence. The heat of the summer night made
his belly slick under the heavy leather. His body knew he
was his own man. He turned and gave his boot heels to
the man and woman pulling from the closet the clothes he
had worn last year as a high-school boy. They didn't even
notice as he went to bed down in the old carriage barn next
to his cycle.

Had Den not fallen asleep, healthy and drained by sex,
he might have heard cutting far away through the silence of
the town's outskirts the sound of Chuck's cycle. The rider
had decided to make a phone call. Even the late-night cop
from the town's bonded protection agency skirted the dark
corner where the lone leatherman in full regalia, cap, shades,
jacket, gauntlets, filthy jeans, and boots, slouched in the
lighted phone booth. Outside in the 3 AM dark, his bike
was kicked up on its stand, waiting, menacing, as the night-
cop's headlights flashed quickly across it and then quietly,
knowing better, disappeared.

The next morning, Den avoided the house. He beat off
in the garage and came on his bike. He had held the front
wheel gripped tight between his kneeling thighs and beat his
meat until he shot white juice over the black tire. He made
a loud point of gunning his bike down the drive and off to

work. He caught a steak-n-eggs breakfast and with a day's butch stubble cruised into Martin's filling station. He said nothing to his boss, but walked straight to the uniform cabinet. He stripped off his leather jacket giving Martin full view of his naked muscular torso. "What's with no T-shirt and no shave?" Martin asked. Den pulled out a green work shirt. He glowered at Martin. "I'll work in the back today," was all he said. He tossed the shirt over the sinew of his shoulder.

Martin knew better than to argue. He had seen Den hyped before. But never so high. Besides, the light shine of sweat beneath the hairs where the boy's smoothly curved spine entered his jeans above his lean buttocks distracted Martin for a moment too long. A lust he didn't understand and that he couldn't tell his wife was swirling in from the back of his head. "I'm gonna have to fire that boy," he said to himself.

Denny worked like a fiend all day, stopping only to speed out of the station on his bike to hit the gym and grab some lunch. Wheeling back toward the station, Den stopped at a corner phone booth. It was the same one Chuck had called from ten hours before. A swastika of dried spit was smeared on the glass. He dialed the office number on the business card he had shoved into his jacket. The extension answered. "You be ready in your workout gear at nine." Den said. "You're on." He hung up the phone. He stepped out of the booth. "You better believe you're on!" He stood with his legs apart and his basket hardening with anticipation.

A girl, a friend of Madonna's, watched Den straddle his leg across his bike and envied the luck of the girl who claimed Den as her guy. She choked as the roar of exhaust exploded and fumed around her. Den had not noticed her, had never noticed her, and would have never missed her if he had.

Chuck slept most of the day. In the late afternoon he drove into Saugatuck and hauled back plenty of beer in the van.

In the light of the bright early evening, coming in through
the west windows of the abandoned farmhouse, he laid out
his gear. From his van he carried in chain, rope, metal clips,
leather thongs, a saddle, two cats-of-nine-tails, several belts,
a hanging harness, a fistfucking sling, a bullwhip, a box of
surgical needles, candles, and a drycell battery attached to a
metal catheter. He laid his tools out carefully, checking padlocks against keys, unknotting a piece of rawhide tangled yet
from last use, slicking every device of bondage and torture
into readiness. Moving his things, he moved his head into
place.

He tapped the high old parlor ceiling to find a heavy
beam. He rolled out an old wooden barrel and stood on it.
He screwed a large iron hook into the beam. A faint dust of
plaster powdered down on him. The veins in his hairy forearm knotted large around his bulldog-cigar USMC tattoo
as he twisted the metal into the hard wood. He made the
last turns with a hammer claw and hitched the hammer into
the loops of his leather jeans. With both fists he grabbed the
hook, pulled down on it tentatively, then swung out surely
from the barrel, hanging and jerking from the beam for a
full minute to test its security. His body, swinging in the
dying sun, elongated. His hands and arms began to ache
carrying the weight of his body and boots. The iron hook cut
sweet into his fingers. A vision of a naked male body hanging
helpless from a pulley on the hook, upside down, made him
harden. He smiled. Satisfied. He dropped to the floor.

He was arranging the ropes on the pulley when the
first cycles roared down the lane and circled the farmhouse.
Chuck walked out onto the porch from which he had sent
Denny off the night before. The outlaw riders, single and
double on bikes, some in full leather, some shirtless in sleeve-
less Levi's jackets shiny with studs, spewed dust and exhaust
circling around the farmhouse. One by one they jacked up
their bikes. They cuffed Chuck in greetings. He broke out

the beer. They were exhilarated by their long run and the prospects of the night. For the next hour more bikers pulled off the highway, singly and in small groups. The brotherhood grew and mingled. They chugged their first beers. They popped their saddlebags for toys they carried into the parlor and laid next to Chuck's equipment.

The seventeenth and last rider, his shirtless torso bulked big with brawn, his jaws lined with a thin cut of beard, his forehead wrapped in a sweatroll of red bandana, pulled into a loud cheer. Before he was off his bike he had two beers shoved at him. He took them both. When Doc arrived, the bikers knew the run was complete. He always started later than the rest so he could trail the crowd. He was an MD and if a biker got into trouble with anything from an exhaust burn to a spill, he was only minutes behind. Doc kicked up his big hog and stomped up the porch to Chuck. "This must be," he said, "the party you called."

After work, Denny had ridden straight home. He walked past his mother preparing supper, walked through his parents' bedroom into the bath, tossed a razor, toothbrush, and soap into a towel. In his own room he pulled a couple of T-shirts from the restraightened bureau and rolled an extra pair of jeans and denim jacket into the old army blanket he had slept on the summer his cousin had forced him out of his bed. He secured his roll with a leather belt. From the false-bottom drawer he pulled the two small physique magazines and burned them in the wastebasket. Now he had the real thing. Thin black smoke spiraled up to the ceiling.

"Denny?" his mother called from the kitchen, "is something burning?"

The paper curled and blackened. Small flames burst up the legs of the muscle men. Heat ate their groins and melted their bellies. Fire crossed their pecs. Their faces dissolved into ash. Denny did not answer his mother.

She started up the stairs. "Is something burning?"

He started down the stairs with his roll. "Yeah," he said. "the house is on fire." As she rushed up the stairs, he escaped any goodbyes. He was on his cycle and in the street before she was at his window knowing he had lied and knowing more: that he was gone for good.

"Storm's blowing up," Den said. He held his head back to catch the wind of the darkening evening sky. Clouds shredded across the horizon. "Storm's coming," Den repeated, "and a hard moon rising." The moon held straight above him, like a plate hung full over the road ahead. Gripping his handlebars and feeling the engine warm between his legs, he knew his long waiting was over. His bike was his liberation. He could breathe. He cruised at top speed past the town's outlying cemetery. It was full of stones for people who were dead and for people who were alive. His family and the Hanrattys already had their markers up, filled in with birth dates and RIP's and only the death date to be chiseled. His brother Rick, or what was left of him, was buried under that stone. "That's all those fuckers are sure of," Den said. "That's all they plan on is dying." He wanted none of it. He had his bedroll on his bike, his bike under him, and he was chasing the moon flatout down the deserted highway. He was no longer waiting for life. He had it. Free.

The rain broke fierce. Den hunched forward against its force and took to a backroads shortcut. He arrived soaked at his M's apartment. He rang the bell. The M opened up. "It's a real gully washer," Den said. The man brought him two huge towels. "No big thing," Den said. "Jeans and T-shirt." The M offered to throw his clothes in his dryer. Den liked the idea. He stripped off his leather jacket. Slow. He teased. He pulled the soggy T-shirt from his shoulders. Rainwater beaded up on his perfect flesh. "Pull off my boots," he said. The man fell to his knees at Den's feet. His hands blackened with wet grease as he pulled the boy's heavy boots from his sockless feet. Den unbuttoned his fly and dropped his jeans to the floor. He stood naked and dominant over the man at his feet.

"You'll be hard on me, Master?" the man asked. His eyes fixed on the thick soft pud of Den's cock.

"Your Master I am."

The man reached for Den's cock; but Den stopped him with a slap in the face. He was a big bear of a man, even kneeling, and he held firm under the slap. "Again, Sir. Please."

Den began to tap the man's cheek. Harder each time. The pats became slaps. "No cock," Den said, "until I'm ready. Understand?"

The man inched back. "May I, Sir, dry your clothes?"

Den kicked his jeans at him. "Hop to it."

The M took the clothes in his teeth and crawled from the room. Den sat on the couch. He toweled his hair dry, then stretched out full length. He dropped the towel across his lean hips. The damp cotton picked up his belly warmth. He dozed for what seemed a minute. He dreamed of warm wet flesh surrounding his cock. He touched his right hand to his left nipple. He woke. Next to the couch knelt the man. His eyes were intent on Den's cock stiffhard under the towel. "Sir, your clothes are dry," he said. Den sat up. He said nothing. The man remained kneeling. Den's cock arrowed out between his legs. Den lit, very deliberately, a cigarette. He inhaled deeply then spewed the smoke into the man's face. "Thanks for drying the clothes," Den said.

"My Master must never thank me."

Den stood up over the big man. "Then thank me properly for thanking you," he said.

The man kneeling eye level with Den's cock had only part of his thank-you said when Den ground out the hot coal of his cigarette on the man's chest.

The rain had stopped when Den and his M walked out to the bike. "This is the kind of rain that starts and stops," the man said.

"You talk too much."

"Yes, Sir."

Den planned to keep the man quiet. The last thing he wanted was to relate personally. They had found each other on one level and in Denny's mind were contracted to stay there. Den was intent on keeping that mouth closed if he had to sew the fucker's lips together. He was out to impress Chuck that he could supply a manslave for them both. In fact, he was thinking more and more in terms of Chuck. Now with their to-be shared M riding on the back of his bike Den felt eager to show Chuck both his bedroll and his masochist. Always there would be M's. But the bedroll was special. A sign he was free. And Chuck was to be the first to know.

Den turned off the highway to the tucked-away farm. The dirt lane had quagged to mire. Far down in the old house Den saw more figures moving in the cloudy moonlight than he had expected. He dragged his bike to a halt and shut it down. His M swung off. Den was pissed. Chuck came out on the porch to meet him. Thumbs up. "Hey! Check out the construction worker you brought," Chuck said.

"Yeah." Den was petulant. "He's a real erector set. Very good at building triangles."

"Easy, Brother," Chuck said. Mystified. "I thought you wanted a three-way."

Denny realized: I want a two-way. You and me. But he said, "Yeah. A three-way."

"Never count your rocks before they're off," Chuck said.

"I never count on anything," Denny lied. He had counted on being free with Chuck, on them being buddy-free together. He didn't like his new feelings. He stomped the mud from his bike boots on the porch. He guessed he was expecting too much too fast. Maybe he was a loner and meant to be. Maybe free was enough. Lone and free. "You're high on something," Den said.

"Just the Holy Trinity," Chuck said crossing himself like a Catholic. "Pot and Acid and Beer." He wanted to cheer Den out of the change he saw. "Come join the Dionysian rites."

"Fucker," Den half-smiled. "Where'd all these guys come from?"

"Here. There. Everywhere. They rose out of a methedrine mist."

"MDA is here to stay," Den's M said.

"Shut-up," Den said. "When my ass needs wiping, then you open your mouth."

Chuck spit off the porch. "They're friends of mine who were headed on a run out of Chicago this weekend. Two thin dimes returned by a midnight telephone operator putting through my collect call changed their previously uncolorful destination. Thank me for corrupting your country innocence."

"I oughta belt you," Den threatened.

"For making you guest-of-honor at your very own special coming-out orgy?" Chuck groped Den's full crotch and kissed him hard on the mouth. Their tongues crossed back and forth over the white fences of teeth. Chuck broke the clench. He had left spit inside Den's mouth. "Come on inside," he said. Den swallowed. Chuck turned to the M standing off by Den's bike. "You too," he said.

Inside the farmhouse the beer flowed. The riders in from the storm were laid back from their ride. Three bikers sat in the middle of the floor surrounded by the joints they were rolling. Others rested in corners. Silent. Smoking. A few leaned against the wall. Hungry eyes. Watching. Watching.

"Where's the action?" Den's M demanded. He saw the possibilities. He goaded. He pushed. "Looks like the Local Leather Ladies Side Saddle Society," he said. "Would whoever owns the Honda 50 outside please move it from blocking the drive."

"Knock its teeth out or gag it," Doc said.

"Do those two come with the place," the M said. He pointed to two men tied up at opposite ends of the room. One, his hands pulled high above his head, tied to a cross-beam, hung, toes touching, naked. His back was well wealed with red-purple belt marks. The other was stretched out cruciform against the wall. His T-shirt had been cut away. Rags of it hung from his shoulders. Barbed fish-hooks pierced both his tits. From the hooks hung small chains decorated like some torturous charm bracelet with lead fishline weights of varying sizes. The weights stretched both his pierced tits down toward his belly.

"Shut-up," Den said. He and Chuck grabbed the M. They tied his wrists and ankles. They dropped him to his belly and pulled his hands towards his heels wrapping the four extremities into a tight hogtie. A sock stuffed into his mouth and secured by a thick strip of rawhide silenced him. "The trouble is," Chuck said, moving Den away from the bound man, "that he maneuvered us into giving him exactly what he wanted. Sort of makes you wonder who's commander and who's commanded."

"I guess a true S would tell every masochist *no*."

"Probably," Chuck said. "But while it may be pure sadism to go into some bar and play Turn-on-and-Turn-down, actually torturing the masochist with the torture he wants or more than he wants has its certain orgasmic compensation. Even though it's not as pure as saying *no*." Chuck popped a beer can. He handed it to Den. Den drank. The farmhouse was surprisingly warm for the damp end of summer. Usually, the last nights of the season, cold came up out of the Michigan fields laying fog across the lowlands and gullies.

A boy about Denny's age moved in on Chuck while Denny drank. It was obvious the two knew each other's bodies intimately. Chuck reached into the boy's unbuttoned denim shirt and manipulated the young brown nipple. Den could imagine it hardening from the faraway look that came into the boy's eyes. Without a word, Chuck reached into his jeans and deftly unscrewed an inhaler. He held it to the boy's left nostril pinching the right one closed. The boy pulled on it heavy. Once. Twice. A third time. He began to moan. He swooned into Chuck. Chuck looked at Den over the helpless boy's shoulder. "Want some?" Chuck offered Den the inhaler.

Den popped another beer. "Why not?" he said. He moved up to the two swaying together. Den's cock fit up against Chuck's solid slab of meat. Den sucked in the smooth popper. He held it up to Chuck. The three of them pushed together like some perfect man-sandwich. But from deep down within the purple corridor of his popper-mind, Den felt the extra body between himself and Chuck. For a moment, the feeling was there again. He didn't want to be so free that he was alone.

"You okay?" Chuck asked.

The threesome broke and the stoned boy wandered off to some other consolation.

"I'm okay." He wanted to tell Chuck his news. He had left home. He had broken the ties. He was his own man.

Chuck put his hand into Den's studded black-leather belt and pulled him along. "Come on. I want you to meet some of these guys." A boy sitting off alone on the sill of a window that had long ago lost its glass waved to the two of them with a joint in his hand. "This is Arrow," Chuck said. Den took the offered joint. He hit it hard and pulled the smoke deep into his big chest. He held it while Chuck pulled on the dope. Finally Chuck said, "Arrow doesn't talk much."

"Arrow doesn't have to," Den said.

"He does look hot." Chuck handed Arrow back his joint. "Too bad he becomes non-verbal when he smokes."

Arrow smiled.

"He's only good," Chuck said, "in a really heavy torture

scene. Preferably western. Arrow's his real name; but I figure he's maybe got some complex about not being the straight Arrow his daddy wanted. At any rate, he's starved for all that true west shit."

Arrow pulled on the roach of his joint. When he raised his big hand to his lips, Den figured he'd grown up working. His hands were rawboned. His gear was real. His jeans were worn white where construction materials had frictioned up his thighs as he lifted cement blocks into position. His torso bulked up to his broad shoulders. His chest was a mat of red hair pouring up out of his cotton undershirt. The white tank top was the kind young Mex pickers wear to transform themselves into low-rider toughs. On his left shoulder above the bicep, a griffin—half lion and half eagle—was tattooed into the freckled skin, so that when the muscles of his arm moved, the mythic animal undulated sensuously.

Arrow handed Den the joint. Den hit it and said, "Great tattoo." Arrow said nothing. He was spaced. "What's the chain around his neck?" Den asked.

Chuck put his hand on Arrow's close-cropped red hair. He was one of those strawberry-roan redheads who come together. Redheads either make it or they don't. This was no freaky carrot-top. Chuck pulled Arrow's head back by the hair. The chain resting in the high fur of his rusty chest hair came into view. "It's the pull chain," Chuck said, "from a toilet at the Gold Coast. Sort of a souvenir. For being best in his class."

"What's the Gold Coast?"

"A sewer in Chicago. A great little leather bar. Arrow is a devotee of the dark night. A slave of Satan. A pissoir. A toilet. A real live Port-O-San. His idea of a holiday is the day after Thanksgiving. Some guys eat turkey. Some turkeys eat shit." Chuck smiled at Denny's disbelief. "There's a lot to learn, my friend. Our tribe does strange things in strange ways and calls them by the best names possible." He pulled Arrow's tongue far out of his mouth. Arrow whimpered with a look of hungry hope in his eyes. Then Chuck dropped him to the floor. He pulled Denny away. "You've a lot to learn," he said.

"Teach me," Den said, "tonight."

"My pleasure. Follow me. Follow Doc. Follow any scene here until you're ready to strike out on your own." Chuck reached into his leather jacket. "Swallow this," he said.

"You're the boss." Denny swallowed the capsule-and-tab cocktail. "For awhile."

"Circulate until you come on. You'll like most of these guys. Check out Doc's action. You'll learn a thing or two fast."

"See you, buddy." Denny took off on a tour of the farmhouse.

Men sat in small groups, drinking and smoking. A guy with long blond Buffalo-Bill hair, and a full mountainman bush of beard, lay back cradled in a leather sling. His feet, laced up knee-high in black pro-wrestling boots, rode in stirrups spread up and in front of him. He crossed his arms on his chest to massage his own nipples. He was built like a fireplug: probably five-foot-eight and two hundred solid pounds. He looked Denny straight in the eye. His tongue came out of the bushy cave of his mouth, licked once around his lips, then headed out and down. He held his mouth open and receptive. He moved his big butt like a pair of warm hams in the sling.

"Fist me," he said. His voice graveled up from deep within the pair of big furry balls hanging between his spread legs. "Come on, man. Grease up your fist. I'll make your hand feel real good. Come on, man. Grease that big fuckin' arm of yours up to the elbow."

Denny moved in between the man's logger thighs. He pushed his basket up against the thick pucker of the waiting asshole. He bumped into the guy. Once. Twice. Slow at first. Nice. Easy. Then harder. The mountainman smiled at him

and laid his head back in the sling. He raised his beefy arms
and held on to the straps of the sling supporting his broad
shoulders. His armpits bushed with thick blond hair. Sweat
poured down his inner biceps. Denny could smell the husky
musk of his sweat in his hairy pits.

"Come on, man." He lifted his head and smiled at
Denny. "Don't tease me, babe. Grease up that muscle-fist
and arm-pump me as deep as you can go."

Denny ground his crotch into the man's butt and steadied the swinging sling. "You want it bad, man? You want my
hard-knuckled fist up your asshole?"

"Do it, man. Please."

Denny leaned in forward between the man's spread legs
and shoved his elbow into the man's mouth. He sucked it
like a hungry arm wrestler with an appetite for biceps and
forearms and fists. Denny pulled the length of his forearm
through the heavy bush of the man's blond beard and across
his eager lips. Then slowly he probed two fingers, then three,
into the man's mouth. He held steady pressure against the
man's teeth, prying his mouth open farther, working his
whole hand into the chunk's face, until his entire fist disappeared into the bushy bearded circle of his mouth. "Feel it,"
Denny said. "You still want it, fucker?" The man's eyes, star-
ing wildly around the muscular forearm protruding from
his mouth, widened in lust. Denny slowly pulled his wet
fist free.

Intensity always draws a crowd.

One of the men moving in to watch hung a Coleman
lantern high on the chain between the mountainman's feet.
The light fell down across him. "Man," Denny said, slowly
unbuttoning his shirt, "you look like some fucking pro-wres-
tler down for the count." Denny stripped to the waist. The
light fell down across his broad shoulders and pecs defining
his washboard abs. They were center ring, Denny and this
big block of a blond bearded man. Neither looked anywhere

but into each others' eyes. Denny held his right forearm out sideways. Arrow, who featured himself the servant of masters, reached into the circle of lamplight, both his hands prepping Denny's fingers, fist, forearm, and elbow with soft white clots of Crisco. Fully greased, Den pulled his arm back, held his forearm upright between his pecs with his fist clenched slightly below his nose. Their eyes met over the big fist. "You still want it? Tell these men how much you want this fucking fist up your asshole. Come on, fucker. Say it."

"I want it, man. I want your fist. I worship your fucking big arms. I want it, man."

The crowd circled in tighter.

Denny lowered his arm, cupped his thumb and pinky together under his three middle fingers, and probed the eager butthole. His fingertips touched the sucking pucker of skin. He eased slowly, expertly, pushing, drawing back, pushing deeper: three fingers, four, the thumb; then back, then in slow, insistent. "Easy. Easy. Easy." Den planted his elbow in the middle of his tight belly. His hand was buried in the warm flesh-tunnel up to the high ridge of knuckle. "Come on. Come on. Give it to me." The mountainman moaned. Someone reached in and held a popper under his nose. His huge chest sucked it in. "That's it," Denny said, "pull it in. Pull it all the way down to your fucking asshole. Inflate your butthole, man." Denny turned his hand slowly clockwise, then counterclockwise. "Come on, buddy. Let me on in. Look at me," Den said. The man opened his eyes. "Give him some more popper." Denny pushed the ridge of his hard fist almost into the ripe ring of butt. "Look at me," Den said. "Keep looking at me. Look at what you wanted working your fine butt over. You wanted it. You got it. Now I want it. Now I'm going to get it." He pushed the ridge of his knuckles past the entry ring of the man's ass. Hungrily, the man moaned as Den's hand slid down the neck of his asshole into the soft envelope of the first chamber. "A perfect fit. My fist and your ass. Like a glove," Den said. He moved his fist back and forth, in and out. "I'm taking your ass, man. I like the feel of your hot butt around my fist. I want to slide in further."

Hands from the dark reached in and clamped the mountainman's tits. He moaned, accepted, refocused, and fell deeper into the scene. The chains to the clamps on his tits stretched out to the darkness, pulling him, adding a rocking motion to the sling. His ass started to tighten and loosen around Denny's fist.

"More?" Denny commanded. He shook his fist inside the hot butt. "More? Come on, man. Ask me for more. Show these fuckers what your ass is made for. Come on. Let me hear it. More...More...More." Denny intoned the hypnotic chant. Dark hands offered more popper. The chains pulled steady pressure on his big blond nipples. "More." Denny started the deep moves into the second chamber. Deeper. Opening the curve. "More." Straightening the deep guts out for a smooth ride all the way to the elbow. "You got it, man," Den said.

The mountainman pushed like a wrestler pinned down center ring on filthy white canvas. He wanted all of Denny inside him. "Give it to me. Shove it in me."

Denny pulled back. Teasing, easing, pleasing with his moves. He was in halfway up his arm. "Feed him some more popper. I'm taking him on home," Denny said. The man's back arched in the gently swinging sling as Den rode on in up to his elbow. "Easy. Easy." Denny took the man's hard cock in his left hand. He worked it slowly up and down while he worked the internal rhythms of his arm deep inside the man's guts.

"Shit!" a voice whispered in the darkness, "you can see his fucking fist poking up through his belly!"

Denny felt a surge of intimacy with the man impaled on his arm. "You're going to cum with me up your ass," he said.

"I'm going to milk your dick while I armfuck your butt." Denny looked up. "Hit him with the popper. Then plenty of pull on his tits." Denny pumped his arm in all the way, then back ten inches, then in, then back, working up through the tight ring of ass, stroking the meaty cock. "I want you to cum," Den said. "I want to feel you cum with my arm inside your ass. I want to feel you clamp down on my arm while I stroke you off."

The man raised his head and looked up at the fuckin' vision of Denny Sargent stripped to the waist, fisting him up to the elbow, and stroking his cock. Denny squinted hard at the man. "I'm spitting on your fucking dick, buddy. I'm stroking your meat. I'm plugging your ass."

Denny hawked up a thick glob of spit from the back of his throat.

The man tensed his whole body.

Denny reared back his muscular neck, thrust his arm full deep into the hot hole, held the fucker's dick tight by the base, and blew a great white hawker to a direct hit on the raging head of the erect rod.

"O shit!" The man's body started to convulse: ass tightening down, dick thrust up. "O shee-it!"

His cum shot like a repeater up and down his body. Clots of thick sperm hit Denny's hairy pecs, mixed with his sweat and started a run down to the dripping tips of his nipples. "Come on," Denny coached. "Come on. Easy. Relax. Easy. Don't push....Give him one more hit....Let me take it from here. Easy. Slow. That's it. Let go. Relax." Denny worked his arm from deep inside the guy's pro-sports belly, slowly, with fixed-rate intensity, finally pulling his fist back down to the chamber just inside the sphincter.

"Take it out. Please." The guy reached his left hand down around his bullballs and locked thumb and forefinger tight around Denny's right wrist.

"Hold on to me," Denny said. "I won't hurt you. Hold

my wrist and guide me out at your own pace." The man's fingers didn't move. "Pull me out," Denny said.

"I can't. Jeez. I fucking can't."

Denny motioned to the dark circle of men. "Hold both his arms back," he commanded.

"Oh no," the man moaned.

"Hit him with popper," Denny said. A look had come over his face. "I'm going back in, all the way to my elbow, and make my exit from there."

The crowd of men circled in and held the big mountain-man's blond body down, steadying his arms and legs and cradling his head. Unseen hands, expert as a puppet master, worked the chains pulling the clamps on his tits, following every move Denny made.

"Come on, man," Denny said. "You've had your fun. Now I want mine." He pushed his fist through the ring of asshole. "Re-entry, fucker." He smoothed it through the first chamber, then finessed it through the deep inner ring that leads further into the belly. "Feel my fucking big arm," Denny said. He paused, held, insistent, then slipped in three more groaning inches. The big blond looked up at Denny with incredible tender thanks. Denny held his depth-thrust for one of those long, silent moments when time stands still. Body heat melted the two men into one connected being.

Then Denny began to breathe again. He unclenched and reclenched his deepfist and started the slow, steady, even, careful slide down and out of the man's butt, suctioning out of him the gut-deep wild animal cries of the serious fist-fucker. The whole movement took only a few seconds. The man was still roaring as Denny stood back to watch him writhe in the many hands holding him.

"Let him go," Denny said. Hands released his feet from the stirrups. His legs slid down the outside of Denny's thighs. The tit clamps disappeared. Denny leaned in over the man, and pulled him up to a sitting position. Their arms wrapped tight around each other.

"You fucking sonuvabitch," the man was sobbing. "You fucking sonuvabitch. Whoever you are, man, I've waited a long time for you." Denny held him in the lamplight while the crowd slipped away into the darkness. Minutes passed between them. "What a fucking thrill," the guy said. He wiped his ass with his towel. "I want to give you my number."

"I got your number already," Denny said.

"So you have," the man said. "So you have." He leaned in close to Denny's ear. "Thanks," he said. "I mean it." And he walked off to another part of the farmhouse wiping his face, unbelieving, dazed, like a man recalling almost forgotten wishes from a long-ago night of shooting stars.

"You do okay for the new kid in town." Doc walked up to Denny. "That was quite a show."

"Is that what it was?" Denny asked. Then he apologized. He was feeling the cocktail coming on. "Sorry," he said. "I guess I like exhibition sex. The big blond's a showboat. World-class. He got off on it. That's what counts."

"What do you get off on?" Doc asked. "That counts for more."

"I got off getting him off," Denny said. He reached his hand out to shake Doc's paw. "Chuck says you're the man to watch when it comes to learning what a real top is all about."

"I have a good time," Doc said. "That's what counts. Not reputation. Only thing reputation gets you is a bad-news fan club of would-be starfuckers. My advice to you, my boy, is: In your life, keep a low profile." He led Denny off to the big old kitchen. "Let me show you something," he said. "Special-order sex."

A wood-burning cookstove warmed the room against the August chill of the Michigan night. Solid hand-hewn beams crossed the high ceiling. Chuck had tied a rope to a beam by a pulley. Denny watched his buddy adjusting the hangman's noose. The big knot was classic true west.

"Fine night for a hangin'," Doc said.

On opposite sides of the room, two men stood facing each other, polar opposites among the gang of men kicked back on boxes and leaning against the walls.

One was Arrow. He stood stripped naked except for a cowboy vest, worn working chaps exposing his dick and balls and butt, and a scuffed pair of White's cowboy boots with underslung riding heels. He waited submissively like a condemned rustler at a lynching. His gloved hands, crossed at the wrists behind his back, were expertly tied with wet rawhide.

The other was Jex-Blake. He was young, grizzled, and wiry. A working cowboy at ease astride a horse in big country or riding a straight-up bike between roadhouse bars. He had a chaw in his cheek, a cup of coffee in his hand, and a pistol holstered low on his right thigh. He was a spur maker by trade, a rover, content to haul saddle and bedroll ranch to ranch. His face was permanently set in the no-shit look that made women and gayboys figure here came a cowboy to straighten out their messy lives. Jex-Blake was an outlaw heartbreaker.

"Arrow has a sweet tooth," Doc whispered to Denny, "for cowboy roughnecks." What he didn't say was that deep down Arrow was from the masochistic subtribe who gladly burn themselves up as sacrifices to their innermost drives and fantasies. What he did say was: "Take this scene in. Trust me. Whatever you see pass between these two, remember that consensual S and M can make a man feel level whatever his baggage. At least for awhile, rough man-to-man sex makes things make sense. It don't matter that eventually breakeven can't be broken." He studied Denny's questioning young face; then kept the final silent secret to himself: maturity is realizing nothing makes sense. "Watch," Doc said. "Observe. Don't judge. You may learn something about the true code of the real west."

Denny's mind had shifted down to soft focus. "Yeah. Sure," he said. Looking at the two intense men, poised on the verge of their scene, Denny understood Arrow's years of lust for the likes of Jex-Blake.

"Tonight's your night." Jex-Blake's dry-as-leather voice rode slow and easy through the thick brush of his big moustache.

"Yessir," Arrow said. His quiet, resigned tone sounded like a man who had seen the ultimate wall and the writing on it: *Wanted Dead or Alive.* He had thrown down his gun and surrendered to a rugged justice he knew would hang him high. His father had been a feedlot boss. He had grown up in a far-off Wyoming town he had thought of no consequence and he had wanted out; but lately something deep within him wanted back, and this was his way home.

Jex-Blake adjusted his six-inch brown-leather wrist cuffs. His gloves, tucked in his belt, hung palm and fingers down over his crotch, looking for all the world like a loose codpiece flopping over the meat bulging through his Wranglers. He radiated the severe, defined Look of a man who is what he is. He stood, legs bowed, a hard rider. A real working cowhand who never heard of an identity crisis. The nape of his redneck had sunbaked to the texture of beef jerky about the time, a dozen or so years before, when he turned twenty. When he swigged on his canteen, he wiped his forearm across his wet mouth. A natural man. Denny could smell his wild uncut dick. But Denny could hardly know of Jex-Blake's two-week drunk the winter before in Ensenada: how a stocky Mex had taken the shit-kicking gringo's cock in his hand and tattooed snake eyes on its pure white head, and the rattles of a snake across the sac of his balls. Denny checked out the cock coiled in Jex-Blake's basket. The bulge was framed by the cutaway crotch circle of his chaparejos made of heavy bullhide to protect his legs from brush and thorns. Jex-Blake was a cowpuncher, more straight than not, but he preferred any good sex scene that fit his natural outlaw style more than he cared if the doggie he was working was man or woman. He treated them both the same.

Always, in the back of Jex-Blake's head, hung a twisted Remington scene, of a naked man confined in a cow chute, zapped to a frenzy with a cattle prod, the gate swinging open, the man running for his life across a muddy horseshit arena, pursued by a leathery roper on horseback, lassoed around the legs, dropped into the mud, jumped by the calf roper leaping off his horse with his lariat lashed to his saddle horn, wrestling the struggling naked man to the ground, and hogtying his wrists to his ankles, leaving him lying on his side in the mud and sawdust and horseshit in under ten seconds, with the crowd calling out for more.

Chuck marched Arrow to the center of the room. He strong-armed the captive toward the two-foot-high wooden crate positioned beneath the noose. He guided Arrow up the one giant step to the lynching platform. Doc had hired Jex-Blake in for a complete scene. "This special trip," Chuck whispered to Arrow, "comes compliments of Doc who knows what you want and gets you what you need." Arrow's knees buckled. Chuck steadied him into direct position under the rope.

"Noose him," Jex-Blake said. He spit the juice from his chaw into his empty coffee mug.

Chuck deftly drew open the loop of the noose. The heavy hemp felt rough through his weather-worn western gloves. With one hand, he reached in, took a leather pinch-hold on Arrow's right tit, and maneuvered him exactly into place. Then with both hands, he dropped the noose slowly over the bound man's head, rope-burning his forehead, nose, and chin with the rough hemp.

"Tighten it up for me," Jex-Blake said. "I want to see that lynch rope pulled real secure around this fucker's outlaw neck."

Chuck fixed the noose in place. The hangman's knot rode where it should, up behind Arrow's left ear.

"Rope his boots tight together," Jex-Blake said. "When this cowboy swings, I want to see him struggle and kick real good." He spit more tobacco juice into his slowly filling coffee mug. "I'm gonna like pistol-whippin' you, cowboy. And there ain't no stoppin' me. I always earn my keep." Jex-Blake moved in toward Arrow. He put his saltsweat gloved hand on Arrow's rising cock. "Work the cowboy up," he said to Chuck. "Then tie the motherfucker off with this rawhide." He pulled a long leather thong from the bottom of his cup. The rawhide was soaked with strong coffee, spit, and tobacco juice. "Wrap the base of his dick and balls tight." Chuck moved in and played expert junior S: stroking and sucking the big redheaded meat up to full hardon.

Denny felt a pang. He wanted Chuck's mouth on his own cock.

Jex-Blake haunched down into his saddlebags and, laying some spur-making equipment aside, pulled a dozen heavy metal rings he'd crafted at his forge. "Start show-dressin' the fucker's balls." He handed the quarter-inch ring bands to Chuck. "I want this cowboy ridin' through the Twelve Gates of Hell." One by one, Chuck slipped first the left nut then the right nut through each ring. He stretched the scrotal sack down to a length that left Arrow swaying in pain on the box. The rings formed a tight neck down the length of the balls. The nuts themselves bulged big and cold and purple from the neck of the twelfth ring. "Let 'im feel them saddle-sore nuts." Denny watched Chuck, without any order from Jex-Blake, shove fresh popper mercifully up to Arrow's nose. Jex-Blake seemed not to notice; he was hard-faced as any rancher out torturing an outlaw rustler.

"Hey," Jex-Blake said to Chuck. "Y'all go on and move back. I take over here." Jex-Blake was twisting a length of barbed wire in his gloved hands. "Whyn't you take this

brandin' iron over and shove it into them wood coals in
the stove." It wasn't a question. Chuck followed the order
exactly.

Doc moved quickly in and snapped a mesh capsule
under Arrow's nose.

Jex-Blake lifted Arrow's steel-necked balls in his left
hand. "Hung like a horse," he said. Then, right-handed, he
wrapped a loop of the barbed wire tight around the base of
his balls and cock. "String the fucker up," he said. "Take up
the slack in that there rope. This here necktie party's about
to begin." His skilled fence-rider's hands took a pliers to the
wire and dug it in deep around the redhaired base of Arrow's
low-slung dick and balls. Then as skillfully as if he were
wrapping a wood post with barbed wire, Jex-Blake wound
the long, hard flesh of Arrow's defenseless cock around and
around, from base to engorged tip. The barbs bit around the
big veins and into the soft flesh. Pricklets of blood trickled
down his dick. It ran slowly down the metal neck of Arrow's
stretched scrotum. It dripped off his balls, reddening the
white pine crate in front of his bound boots.

In continuing, swelling panic, Arrow felt the noose
growing steadily tighter around his throat and neck. Hanged
by the neck until dead. Death by hanging. Feedlot ropes.
His dad knew how to handle outlaws.

Jex-Blake's face was intent, precise, and hard-bitten.

Denny through his haze saw men taking long strokes on
their meat: some of them cuming at the mutual extremity
of Arrow's desires and Jex-Blake's actions. He freed his own
cock and felt it hardening in his hand. Almost instantly,
a man in a piss-soaked jock glided in from the darkness
and knelt at Denny's crotch. He sucked the cheesy uncut
head into his mouth. To Denny everything felt right. Late
nights in his parents' house, he had read and dreamed about
extremities. He knew he was witnessing his own personal
baptism into the group's celebration of the ritual sweat and

blood and fire of hard-balling mansex. The deep, wet mouth slowly, sensuously worked the head and shaft of his cock. The skillful sucking maintained him hot and balanced as Jex-Blake's sure moves dogged Arrow deeper and deeper into the box canyon of pain.

The noose tightening on Arrow's neck kept his tortured cock and balls hard. His head drifted in and out of the scene. The vision of Jex-Blake's classic cowboy Look tripped him back to Wyoming. To the hard-drinking last night of the Gillette rodeo. His dad's feedlot gang was mixing it up with the local working cowboys. Having a helluva time. Slapping the fourteen-year-old Arrow on the back of his quilted down vest. A wirey cowboy arm hung round his young shoulders. The close-in whiskey face of a cowboy giving Arrow confidential advice every man at the table could hear. Arrow was having the time of his young life.

Arrow's dad sat opposite him. Rolling himself one-handed smokes. Drinking with the best of them. Proud the way his son handled himself. Arrow, not quite sure what to do, but quite sure he was exactly where he wanted to be, made his moves slow. He moved the way the men in the bar moved, but he moved a beat behind them. Not sure what to say, he listened. He was a perfect ear for whiskey talk. Under the table his hand covered the mound of hard boycock in his jeans. Jawing and drinking a few beers with his dad's pards was something he'd been waiting for.

The rest of that particular night was the sort of history that never gets recorded, but's never forgot either: how three fairground fellows, all rodeo cowboys, paraded into the bar duded up in straw hats and slick boots and silver trophy buckles, fighting drunk and bragging about their rides.

Almost faster than Arrow could follow, the three show cowboys started a punch out with the barful of working cowboys in a brawl they could never win.

The biggest one escaped when Arrow's dad kicked his ass

through a window; he ran off into the night on his silver-toed
boots. The middle-size one had a terminal glass jaw: a swift
uppercut thrown by the cowboy who'd sat with his heavy
arm around Arrow's shoulders cold-cocked him good. Later
he revived fast when the barkeep dragged him across the
floor to the john and shoved his face into the cold pisswater
toilet.

The third rider was one tough little man, a hard-muscled
cockfighter, good, very good, in a bare-knuckle scrap. It took
four or five of the local cowpunchers to make short work of
him. The boys wrestled him like a steer to the wood floor.
Arrow's dad dragged the little maverick by the scruff of his
neck out the door. The feedlot posse crowded in behind
them, deviling the downed man, kicking and spitting on
him, spurring him on toward the dark back of the feedlot. A
roper dropped a lasso tight around his neck. They dragged
him through a small corral. "Eat dirt, asshole!" They pushed
his mouth into the dust. His stash came up caked with mud.
A boot on the back of his neck shoved his face into a fresh
steaming horse-pie. Arrow had never seen anything like that;
he had never heard laughter like that.

They pulled the shit-covered outsider to a railroad X-sign.
Arrow watched them lift the drunken cowboy in his filthy
satin shirt and torn jeans up against the railroad cross. They
spreadeagled him to the four heavy-beamed wooden arms.
He was roped tight and secure. The men passed around a
bottle of whiskey. Arrow's dad handed the bottle to his son.
Arrow raised the bottle to his lips and pulled a long burning
swig.

He could never forget that moment: looking at his father
who had led these men, tasting his first whiskey, feeling
the pressure of his hardon in his jeans, seeing the crucified
cowboy hanging on the railroad cross, helpless and drunk
and howling at the full Wyoming moon low on the horizon
behind him.

Arrow's dad put his big hand on his son's shoulder and guided him behind the other men out of the feedlot and back to the bar. "That's how," he said, "you treat them rodeo show-circuit fags."

S and M passion rises out of far off nights like that, fueled by memory, driven by dick beyond any logic.

Jex-Blake pulled a soft deerskin tobacco pouch from his vest pocket. Never taking his squint off Arrow, he rolled himself a cigarette, struck a light in his cupped hand, and took a long, meditative drag. "Hoist 'im up higher," he said. Chuck wrapped the rope around his gloved hand and pulled Arrow up to the toes of his boots. Denny liked the way his leather buddy moved. Chuck fastened the rope end to the leg of the big cast iron stove. Arrow's breath came in shorter hits. His eyes took on a wild look. A vein pulsed out on his forehead.

Jex-Blake lifted a silver spur of his own making from his saddlebags. He slowly, tantalizingly drew the circle of rowels across the palm of his glove. The sharp points left a trail of needle marks in the soft leather. Arrow eyed him with a wild look. Jex-Blake's butt of cigarette hung on his lower lip. He moseyed, menacing, on in toward Arrow. He took three deliberate steps toward the wooden crate. Raising his bowed leg like he was mounting some wild stallion he had every intention of breaking, he lifted himself full height up on the platform.

For the first time, Jex-Blake and Arrow were eye-to-eye.

Slowly Jex-Blake folded the flaps of Arrow's vest back. He exposed Arrow's pecs. He ran his gloved hand nipple to nipple through the thick strawberry-roan fur. Arrow looked down in fear, choking himself. He knew the soft strokes of the leather glove would give way to the deep plowing of the sharp needle rowels. And what he expected, happened. Jex-Blake planted the rowels hard against Arrow's chest. With the full strength of his arm, he pulled the spur hard,

crisscrossing Arrow's pecs with pinpoint bloodlines. There
were no screams. What surprised Denny were Arrow's pain-
fully furrowed brows squinched over his eyes that looked to
cry more from ultimate gratitude than pain.

Jex-Blake, without taking his eyes from Arrow's face,
said to Chuck: "Hand me the bridle."

Denny had never seen such a head harness. Once made
for horses, it was reworked to mansize. In Jex-Blake's hands,
the straps and buckles locked fast around, above, and below
Arrow's head. The super-tight harness cinched his face and
skull, squeezing, distorting his features from man into animal. His head was completely harnessed except for the metal
bit that hung down with one last strap alongside his mouth.

"Hand it to me," Jex-Blake said. Chuck covertly palmed
a strange, large nugget into Jex-Blake's glove. He gave Arrow
a long hit of popper, and stepped back to the sidelines. This
time Chuck stood next to Denny who pushed the tireless
cocksucker off his dick. He put his arm around Chuck's
shoulder. Chuck put his hand on Denny's cock.

"Open wide," Jex-Blake said.

Arrow stared disbelieving at him through the tight straps
of the harness. He would not, could not, open his mouth.

"Inch the rope up a couple more notches," Jex-Blake
said. Unseen hands followed his orders. The noose tightened
around Arrow's neck. "I'm hungry for a hanging," Jex-Blake
said. He put one gloved hand to Arrow's mouth to pry it
open; with the other he slipped the huge golden nugget of
horseshit well back on Arrow's tongue. Arrow tried to spit,
but could not.

For the first time, Jex-Blake smiled with some satisfac-
tion. "You hold it, boy. You understand?"

Arrow's nostrils flared. He understood.

"And to make sure," Jex-Blake said, "I'm gonna strap this
bridle bit tight as I can back between your teeth." Deliberate
as his drawl, he forced the bit in place, distorting the lines

of Arrow's mouth, exposing his equus teeth, depressing his tongue flat under the horse muck, twisting his facial features into some weird tortured mask of submission. Denny watched Arrow's throat, tight inside the noose, convulse in struggling swallowing motions, as his saliva juiced up the stallion nugget with nowhere to go but down his belly.

"Jesus," Denny whispered.

Chuck held him steady by his cock. He leaned into Denny's ear. "You're seeing one man's version of heaven," he said.

Jex-Blake pulled off his worn leather gloves. Arrow's eyes bugged wild behind the tight squeeze of harness. Jex-Blake paused. A dark hand reached popper to Arrow's nose. He breathed in deep. Then Jex-Blake, with both gloves in one hand, began to slap leather across Arrow's bound face. Hard. Alternating the blows: five to the face; five to the wired cock and balls. Then harder: ten, fifty, a hundred.

Denny lost count as Chuck stroked his dick.

Blood ran from Arrow's nose. It drained through his moustache into his mouth, mixing with his saliva, melting the horse nugget. Jex-Blake ran his finger across Arrow's exposed teeth. He rubbed the mix of blood, spit, and horseshit together on his fingertips. He snorted his hand. "Corral soup," he said. Then, accurate as a sharpshooter, he aimed a long brown spit of his Red Man chaw straight into Arrow's mouth. "Hang 'im up another notch," Jex-Blake said. Arrow was near to blacking out, more from passion than pain.

Denny watched Doc, standing on duty next to Chuck, reach for ammonia capsules.

"Hand me my reins," Jex-Blake said.

Doc went for the leather gear. The move gave him ease to move in and hit Arrow up with a double blast of ammonia and popper. Doc's boiler-maker screwed Arrow's tripping eyes back into reality focus.

Arrow watched Jex-Blake's hands reaching toward his tits. He felt the heavy-toothed clamps bite deep into his nipples. The head of his wire-bound cock grew larger. He felt the dried horse-lather weight of the leather reins attached to the clamps. He breathed the exhale of Jex-Blake's hard smile as the cowboy took both reins in his hand and stepped down from the platform, pulling the reins taut as he backed away from the bound man hanging by the neck in agony. "Ride 'em, cowboy," was all he said as he handled the reins, riding Arrow's tits, hellbent for leather. Arrow swayed back and forth from the pull, guided left, then right, like a horse under an expert rider's reins.

Screaming came now, from deep within Arrow's cock and balls, from the pure torture of the reins tearing his tits raw; but the sound of his screaming was muffled by the big ball of hot horseshit held in place in his mouth by the harness bit.

Denny noticed that the head of Arrow's wildly swinging dick was beginning to drip with pre-cum lube.

"Beautiful," Chuck whispered. "Man, you're beholding ecstasy."

"Ready?" Jex-Blake spoke to Doc and handed him the reins. "Give the boy whatever he needs. But keep a tight rein in on his tits."

Doc walked up to Arrow and dosed him again, this time with pure ammonia; he wanted him alert and up.

Jex-Blake moved to the stove and pulled the red-hot branding iron from the coals. He walked slowly around the circle of men in the room, cooling the iron down from cooking-red to branding-black. Then he walked straight up to Arrow. He inched the hot iron in close enough that Arrow could smell his moustache singeing. He could feel the horse bit heating up across his tongue. For the second time, something like a scream came from deep inside his throat.

Jex-Blake looked Arrow in the eye; Arrow could see nothing but the branding iron. "Tonight's your night, cowboy," Jex-Blake said.

He pulled the branding iron away and walked slowly behind Arrow's back.

Doc moved in for one more boiler-maker hit.

"Pull hard on them reins," Jex-Blake said. "And you over there, hang 'im! Lynch 'im! Make 'im swing!"

Everything worked at once.

Arrow, pulled forward by his tits and lynched at the neck, felt his feet leave the platform. He was hanging by his neck, hands tied behind his back, boots roped together, thrashing in total final suffocating agony. Inside he was dying. His thrashing, twitching body began to slump from his elongating neck. Arrow was headed down a long dark corridor toward a blinding purple light. Heading toward Wyoming. He felt his ass contract and shudder under a strange coup de grace: Jex-Blake, with all the might of both his arms, swacked a 2x4 with unbearable force across Arrow's hanging butt. Behind its stunning slam came the hot branding iron sizzling through the fresh bruise into his naked right cheek. He was not dying. He was in searing pain. A wild, burning, living scream shot not from his mouth but from deep inside his branded ass, through his ring-stretched balls, and out the end of his barbed-wire cock.

His seed showered the room. Men fell on their knees beneath him to receive it. Denny's face dripped with sweat mixed with clots of Arrow's cum. The sweet smell of seared flesh filled the dark room. As fast as the finale built, the scene was over. Arrow was dropped down on the platform: hands releasing his neck, unharnessing his head, slapping his face, plying the barbed wire off his dick, slipping the greasy rings off his nuts, salving his branded butt. He lay in Doc's arms convulsing in exhausted passion.

Doc motioned Jex-Blake over to the platform. He hunkered down next to Arrow. Doc lifted Arrow's head. Arrow opened his eyes.

"Thank the man," Doc said.

Arrow could not speak. The last of the horse nugget stuck in his mouth.

"Swallow it," Jex-Blake said. "Swallow it." He began to stroke slowly on Arrow's throat. "Swallow it," he soothed. "Thank me by swallowing."

Arrow mustered what strength he had left. He looked Jex-Blake directly in the face, and with the pressure of the cowboy's leather-gloved hand on his throat he obediently swallowed.

"Shit, Chuck," Denny said. "You better take your hand off my dick or I'm gonna shoot."

"Not yet, brother," Chuck said. "Not yet." He gently folded Denny's dick back inside his 501s. "Follow me," he said. They left the kitchen with Arrow laid across Doc's lap like a pagan Pieta.

In the ramshackle parlor, Chuck pointed Denny toward a completely mummified body tied against a post. The mummy head was covered by a second layer of a tight rubber latex hood. A single breathing tube protruded from where the mouth once rattled on. "Recognize him?" Chuck asked. Denny shook his head. He hadn't realized that dozens of other scenes had also played on into the late night. "That's the loud-mouthed photographer dude you brought out here tonight on your bike." Denny laughed; he had lost interest in the jerk the more he talked, and he was glad that some other guys had found him worth their amusement. "All the dude's got going for him," Chuck said, "is that big piece of meat." The man's hardon, protruding through the mummy wrap, was tied around the corona of the head with a black-leather strap. From that, on a short chain, hung a 14-D black-leather Georgia engineer boot.

"Let's take a leak," Chuck said. He led Denny up to the bound cock. Together they took out their dicks and pissed into the leather neck of the boot, adding the weight of their thick, steaming streams. The mummified figure tried to move. The gallon of piss hung heavy from his bound cockhead. "Keep pissing," Chuck said. Denny liked the watery contest. He took hold of Chuck's cock, aiming it bull's-eye into the boot. Chuck reciprocated. They stood together, arms around their shoulders, holding each other's pissing cocks, watching the boot foam up to the top and begin to overflow, running down the elastic bandages of the immobile mummy. Each took for the other the final honors of mutually shaking the last pissdrips from their mansize cocks. "The dude got even more than he bargained for," Chuck said. "With no skin off your nose." He smiled his killer smile at Denny. "I'm glad," he said, "that the night's gone the way it's gone. We've got some energy left for each other."

That kind of talk turned Denny on. "Maybe we should, uh, have a talk...or something," Denny said.

Chuck led him out to the porch, down the steps, and across the yard to his private van. Overhead, the white light of the setting moon hung low in the west over Lake Michigan. At least two hours of darkness remained before this Midwestern summer's night mixed with the predawn eastern rose of the rising sun. "Climb on in," Chuck said.

Denny hesitated.

"Come on," Chuck said, "this is a van parked in the Michigan dunes south of Saugatuck. Not a cottage for two by the sea. Relax. It's okay. I know you want action more than a lover. You're fuckin' eighteen, built like twenty-five. I can respect that."

Denny smiled and climbed on into the dark berth of the van. In his lightly stoned head, visions collided of his brawny dad, of Stoney, of Sam, of his first fuck with Chuck, of the blond bearded mountainman with the insatiable ass, of Doc and Arrow and Jex-Blake. He lay his head back on Chuck's bedroll and said nothing.

Chuck lay down beside him. "I know what is, is, man. I also know that what you're looking for is looking for you.

I mean, I know that for me. And we seem to be, well, a lot alike." He laid his curly head down on the fresh piss-wet muscular crook of Denny's arm. He put his hand down on the fresh piss-wet of Denny's denim basket. "I don't want no lover either." They lay together, relaxing, half-dreaming, each wandering in his own thoughts and plans.

Denny turned on his side and faced Chuck. "What we need, buddy, is some serious shut-eye."

"You want to cum?" Chuck asked.

"My head's been cuming all fuckin' night, man. I can sleep. How about you?"

"I can wait till morning," Chuck said. He nosed in through Denny's sweaty armpit and tongued down on his right pec and nipple. "I'd like to wake up with a raging piss hardon, and fuck it slow up your nice tight ass, and then piss deep inside your guts."

"So," Denny said, "maybe I want to wake up with a raging piss hardon, and fuck it slow down your nice tight throat, and then piss deep inside your guts."

"You might say," Chuck said, "that some of what we're looking for has just found us."

Denny wondered. He had played turn-on and turn-down at Mr. Martin's station so long that his mouth could hardly say what his whole muscular body honestly wanted. "What say," Denny said, "we just sleep here tonight, holding on to each other, and maybe wake up in the morning the best pair of fuck-buddies the world has ever seen?"

"Sounds good to me," Chuck said. "You're the best man I ever did see."

"And I like you. I like the way we treat each other. But maybe I like you, man, because I know you know how to get me out of Michigan. If you don't mind that angle, shoot, partnered up, who knows what hell we might raise. Look, I got my bike. You got your van and your bike. You got Chicago connections coming out of the ass." Denny touched

Chuck's chin. "Don't let my enthusiasm sound like I'm trying to use you," he laughed, "because it's more than using
you. If I use you, you can use me till you use me up. I swear.
My honest-to-God bottomline is all my life I've been waiting
to give as good as I get."

"That's mutual," Chuck said. "And after Chicago, how
about California?"

"California," Denny said. "That has a real nice ring to
it."

"Hey," Chuck said, "this isn't just our late-night drugs
talking, is it?"

Denny laughed and pulled Chuck to him, leather against
leather, man-to-man, and stuck his tongue deep down his
throat. "Swallow my spit, man," he said.

Chuck swallowed, and then thrust his own tongue into
Denny's mouth. "Eat my spit, pard." He served up a healthy
hawker. "And love it."

Denny swallowed half. "Partners," Denny said. Spit
returned.

"Brothers," Chuck said. Spit served.

"Hermanos," Denny said. Spit returned.

"Compadres," Chuck said. Spit swallowed.

"Fuckbuddies," Denny said. Spit served.

"Friends," Chuck said. Mixed spit returned and mutually swallowed.

"In a free-for-all," Denny said. "Free to come. Free to go."
He pulled Chuck in hard against him. "And free to fuck."

"Sounds sort of like we're riding off into the sunset
together," Chuck said.

"As long as the road's good and mutual for us both."

"Never rode a freeway yet that didn't have an off ramp
when needed." Chuck said.

Denny wrapped his legs around Chuck's legs. Their
naked pecs touched nipple to nipple. Their cocks were grind-
ing into each other. They wrestled in muscled-arm embrace.

Chuck pushed his thick moustache against Denny's upper lip and whispered, "Chicago's sounding pretty good." Denny chewed on Chuck's moustache and whispered back. "And California's sounding even better."

There wasn't much sleep for them that night.

Arising in the last hour of darkness, before the others stirred about the farm site, they gathered up their gear, loaded both bikes into the van, and with the gold-bright dawn warm on their backs, they pursued their mutual shadow westward.

Also by Jack Fritscher

Fiction Books

Leather Blues, A Novel of Leatherfolk, 1969, 1972, 1984

Corporal in Charge of Taking Care of Captain O'Malley and Other Stories, 1984, 1999, 2000

Stand By Your Man and Other Stories, 1987, 1999

Some Dance to Remember: A Memoir-Novel of San Francisco 1970-1982, 1990, 2005

What They Did to the Kid: Confessions of an Altar Boy, 1966, 2002

The Geography of Women, 1998

Titanic: Forbidden Stories Hollywood Forgot, 1999

Sweet Embraceable You: Coffee-House Stories, 2000

Jacked: The Best of Jack Fritscher, 2002

Stonewall: Stories of Gay Liberation, 2009

Non-Fiction Books

Love and Death in Tennessee Williams, 1967

Popular Witchcraft: Straight from the Witch's Mouth, 1971, 2004

Television Today, 1972

Mapplethorpe: Assault with a Deadly Camera, 1994

Mapplethorpe: El fotographo del escandalo, 1995

Gay San Francisco: Eyewitness Drummer—A Memoir of the Sex, Art, Salon, Pop Culture War, and Gay History of Drummer Magazine, 2008

Photography Book

Jack Fritscher's American Men, London, UK, 1995

Writing in Other's Books

Gay Roots: Twenty Years of Gay Sunshine: An Anthology of Gay History, Sex, Politics, and Culture, Winston Leyland, 1991

Vamps and Tramps: New Essays, Camille Paglia, 1994

Leatherfolk: Radical Sex, People, Politics, and Practice, Mark Thompson, 1991

Mystery, Magic, and Miracle: Religion in a Post-Aquarian Age, Edward F. Heenan, 1973

Challenges in American Culture, Ray B. Browne, 1970

Best Gay Erotica 1997, Douglas Sadownick and Richard Labonté, 1997

Best Gay Erotica 1998, Richard Labonté, 1998

Chasing Danny Boy: Powerful Stories of Celtic Eros, Mark Hemry, *1999*

Bar Stories, Scott Brassart, 2000

Best of the Best Gay Erotica, Richard Labonté, 2000

Friction 3, Austin Foxxe & Jesse Grant, 2000

The Leatherman's Handbook, "Gay History Introduction," 25th Anniversary Edition, Larry Townsend, 2000

Rough Stuff, Simon Sheppard & M. Christian, 2000

Bear Book II, Les Wright, 2001

The Burning Pen: Sex Writers on Sex Writing, Simon Sheppard, 2001

Tales from the Bear Cult, Mark Hemry, 2001

Twink, John Hart, 2001

Bears on Bears, Ron Suresha, 2002

Censorship: An International Encyclopedia, Derek Jones, 2002

Friction 5, Jesse Grant and Austin Foxxe, 2002

Tough Guys, Bill Brent & Rob Stephenson, 2002

Best American Erotica 2003, Susie Bright, 2003

Kink, Paul Willis & Ron Jackson, 2003

First Hand, Tim Brough, 2006

Country Boys, Richard Labonté, 2007

Homosex: Sixty Years of Gay Erotica, Simon Sheppard, 2007

Best Gay Bondage Erotica, Richard Labonté, 2008
Best Gay Romance 2008, Richard Labonté, 2008
Best Gay Romance 2009, Richard Labonté, 2009
Special Forces: Gay Military Erotica, Phillip MacKenzie, Jr.,
   2009
Muscle Men, Richard Labonté, 2010
Hot Daddies, Richard Labonté, 2011

Writing in Scholarly Journals
"William Bradford's *History of Plymouth Plantation*,"
   The Bucknell Review
"Religious Ritual in the Plays of Tennessee Williams,"
   Modern Drama
"2001: A Space Odyssey,"
   The Journal of American Popular Culture
"The Boys in the Band in *The Boys in the Band*,"
   The Journal of American Popular Culture
"*Hair*: The Dawning of the Age of Aquarius,"
   The Journal of American Popular Culture

Photographs Appearing in Other's Books
*The Arena of Masculinity: Sports, Homosexuality, and the
   Meaning of Sex*, Brian Pronger, London, 1990
Narrow Rooms, James Purdy [cover], London, 1997
Ars Erotica: An Encyclopedic Guide, Edward Lucie-Smith,
   London, 1998
Adam: The Male Figure in Art, Edward Lucie-Smith, Lon-
   don, 1998

Writing and Photography in Magazine Culture
Jack Fritscher's fiction, essays, and photography appear
regularly or variously in the following magazines: *Drum-
mer, International Leatherman, Honcho, Thrust, Harrington
Gay Men's Fiction Quarterly, The James White Review, Vice,
Unzipped, Leather Times: Journal of the Leather Archives &*

Museum, The Leather Journal, Skin, Skinflicks, Dungeonmaster, Inches, In Touch, Checkmate, Powerplay, Bear, Classic Bear Annual, Son of Drummer, Bunkhouse, Mach, Man2Man Quarterly, Uncut, Foreskin Quarterly, Hombres Latinos, Just Men, Stroke, Rubber Rebel, Eagle from *The Leather Journal, Hippie Dick, Gruf, William Higgins' California, Men in Boots Journal, GMSMA Newsletter, Hot Ash Hot Tips, The California Action Guide, Adam Gay Video Guide, Dan Lurie's Muscle Training Illustrated, Hooker, Expose, California Pleasure Guide, The Bay Area Reporter, BARtab,* and others.

For further bibliography and gay history, visit
JackFritscher.com

CPSIA information can be obtained at www.ICGtesting.com
Printed in the USA
LVOW12s1916090813

347197LV00001B/39/P